FOLLOWING

FAKE

MAN

FOLLOWING
FAKE
MAN

BARBARA WARE HOLMES
illustrations by Sarah Hokanson

ALFRED A. KNOPF ✦ NEW YORK

All of the characters and events in this book are fictional.

THIS IS A BORZOI BOOK PUBLISHED BY ALFRED A. KNOPF

Text copyright © 2001 by Barbara Ware Holmes
Illustrations copyright © 2001 by Sarah Hokanson
Jacket illustration copyright © 2001 by Tom Voss
All rights reserved under International and Pan-American Copyright
Conventions. Published in the United States of America by Alfred A.
Knopf, a division of Random House, Inc., New York, and simultaneously
in Canada by Random House of Canada Limited, Toronto.
Distributed by Random House, Inc., New York.
KNOPF, BORZOI BOOKS, and the colophon are registered trademarks of
Random House, Inc.
www.randomhouse.com/kids
Library of Congress Cataloging-in-Publication Data
Holmes, Barbara Ware.
Following Fake Man / Barbara Ware Holmes ;
illustrations by Sarah Hokanson.
p.   cm.
Summary: During his summer in Maine, twelve-year-old Homer,
together with his new friend Roger, is determined to find the truth about
himself, his long-dead father, and a mysterious costumed man.
ISBN 0-375-81266-0 (trade) — ISBN 0-375-91266-5 (lib. bdg.)
[1. Father—Fiction. 2. Artists—Fiction. 3. Maine—Fiction. 4. Mystery
and detective stories.] I. Hokanson, Sarah, ill. II. Title.
PZ7.H7337 Fo 2001
[Fic]—dc21   00-051461

Printed in the United States of America
May 2001
10 9 8 7 6 5 4 3 2

To my mother,
Dorris Savoy,
and my mother-in-law and stepfather-in-law,
Margaret and David Van Name
—BWH

FOLLOWING
FAKE
MAN

1

"This kid was nursed on a pickle," Madeleine liked to tell anyone who would listen. Meaning me, of course, Homer Winthrop. "Nursed on a pickle and weaned on prune juice." She said it now, catching a look at my face in her rearview mirror.

Ha ha.

Well, so what? I enjoyed being a pickle. I enjoyed sulking and not talking. I planned to not talk all the way into Maine. But it was going to be hard, I saw as we crossed the bridge into the state. This place was already looking interesting. The river was named the Piscataqua, probably after Indians.

"Pis-CAT-aqua," I said accidentally. "Or Pisca-TA-qua. Or, no, PIS-cat-aqua."

"Gesundheit," Madeleine answered.

Don't talk, I reminded myself. I closed my eyes.

"Homer, are you all right?" This was my mother speaking. She'd been spinning around in her seat to stare at me about once every twenty minutes since we'd left Boston.

I didn't answer, just opened my eyes very wide. I'd done this the whole trip, which was making my eyeballs feel kind of funny, like I might be doing them damage. I wasn't, of course. My mother would have said so if this were the case. She lived to say things like that. Now Madeleine (latest in our long line of housekeepers, drivers, general all-round-slaves-to-my-mother) was different. When she caught me popping my eyeballs, she just popped hers right back. *That* was a sight worth seeing. Hers were so poppy you just sort of waited, thinking they'd bounce over the seat and into your lap.

My mother sighed. I closed my eyes again. We started and stopped and started and stopped and drove for a while and then stopped again.

"Lord have mercy," Madeleine said. "At least in Boston the traffic jams while it's still moving!"

"Oh, Madeleine, I believe that's a contradiction in terms."

And there you had it—the perfect example of what was wrong with my mother. Let Madeleine say something perfectly clear and interesting, and along would come Dr. Winthrop, *the linguist*, to pick it apart and take all the fun out of it. My mother heard words instead of what a person was saying. Why bother to talk? I wanted to tell Madeleine, but that'd be like telling a boat not to float.

I opened my eyes and stared at the back of my

mother's head: a circle with a bun in the middle, all perfect and neat. I stared at the back of Madeleine's: a boingy-haired triangle sticking out to the tips of her shoulders. A bird could be living in there. A twittery, fluttery bird. I believe those two heads told you all you needed to know. If I were drawing those heads, I'd—

"Oh my," my mother said suddenly. "Oh my, oh my." Her hand tapped away at her chest like one of those fluttery birds.

"Oh my what?" Madeleine asked. "You all right over there?"

My mother nodded, but her hand went on tapping. Madeleine shot her a look. I shot her a few myself. Not much fluttered my mother. In fact, nothing fluttered my mother except her headaches, and those were more like a knockout punch.

"Here's where we turn, Madeleine," she said suddenly, her voice sort of shaky and squeaky like I'd never heard it before. "We're on the peninsula. Herring Cove is right at the end of it." I studied the back of her head. A lock of hair had popped out of the bun, and now her neck looked different. Ridges had appeared at the base of it. Something major was up. Something bigger than a vacation—something *much* bigger. Which I should have known since my mother did not take vacations. Since my mother did not usually spin in her seat.

"Why are we coming here?" I asked, forgetting my vow of silence.

My mother was silent a long time. The neck sprouted a row of speckles. Or maybe it was the glow of the afternoon sunlight streaming in through the windows and over her seat that was making it look that way. Colors seemed different in Maine. The very air looked different, if air could look. I threw this thought in the suitcase I called my brain for thinking about later. Right now I was too busy boring holes in the back of my mother.

"*Why* are we coming?" I asked again in a voice that could not be ignored. Well, it could, but it better not be. I was tired of being ignored. Tired of being my usual self. The one that scowled but kept his mouth shut.

"I—We—I—have business regarding a house," my mother said finally. "My—*our* house."

This made my jaw drop, it was such a surprise.

I guess to Madeleine, too. "You mean the house we're going to is your own personal property?"

"Yes, Madeleine. It is."

"And I have been in that house before." I announced this without even thinking or knowing for sure it was true. Except that I did know. I could feel it, like there was this cloud floating through the backseat carrying this feeling of truth. What truth? That I was coming *back* to a place I'd been before.

That feeling just floated over me and sat there, being wavery but true.

My mother even admitted it. "Yes. We came here when you were a baby."

Which meant when my father was living? I stared at the back of her head. It sat up now, on top of an ostrich neck. The very sight of it made me crazy. For the first time in my life I was going to a place where my father had been, and my mother hadn't bothered to tell me?

All of a sudden, this hole opened up inside of me, that's the only way to explain it. A hole where my father should be. I guess the hole had always been there. But now it opened up.

And it's weird about holes inside you, how they can make you feel, well, *full*. Full and empty at the very same time.

Nobody talked after this. Not even Madeleine.

2

We rode along being silent. Me being mad. Because here's the thing.

I used to have a father. Well, okay, everyone has a father. But most people know stuff about theirs. Details, like: What does (did) he eat for breakfast? Which baseball teams did he like? What were his favorite hobbies? I didn't know any one of those things. I only knew this: My father was a neurologist who'd died of a neurological illness. Which was a "sad irony"—all my mother would say about that. I was two when the sad irony happened.

Okay, maybe I knew a few other things. If I asked a very specific question such as "Where was my father born?" my mother would answer "Cleveland." But that was all. She'd never add "and he was so happy there." Or, "He sure did hate his parents." Sometimes she wouldn't answer at all. She'd just stand perfectly still and stare at me like I was making her think of something, but she wasn't saying what. Like her mind was whirring and memories were flying, but stand back, because they were private. I'd given up asking questions.

Which meant I had to give up on knowing my father, because how else was I going to find out? Since my father had died, I'd never been to one place he had been or met one person who'd known him. Not his relatives—cousins, I think—who lived someplace far away. Not my grandparents, who were dead. Only my mother, who wasn't talking.

But my father had been *here*. He'd driven right down this road and over this very hill. He had probably seen that house, and that one. The thought gave me the weirdest feeling, like my father had reached out his hand and touched me and my arm was still warm where his hand had been. For the first time ever, my father felt real to me. Like a person who'd lived and breathed.

"Wow," I whispered.

"This is it!" croaked my mother. "We're in Herring Cove."

The road dipped, rose up, passed a row of houses, two churches, a post office, and right there in front of us was the sea. Man, I couldn't look around fast enough. This place was too cool for words. Look at the boats out on the water. Look at—

"Law, look at the cars," Madeleine clicked her tongue.

It was true. To our left was a sea of parked cars,

and more cars were on the move, boxing us in from behind and coming toward us as we rounded a steep downhill corner.

"People park here to go out to the islands," my mother said weakly. She was huffing and puffing, like she'd run all the way from Boston. "But it is all changed. Oh, look at the buildings along the water. They must block the view from the house." She tsk-tsked and clutched at the front of her shirt.

I looked. A general store. A marina. A fish store. A public landing, where people were pulling kayaks out of the water. All changed, my mother had said. Changed since my father? Yes, but it couldn't really have *all* changed, and I loved it anyway, for its own self, even separate from my father. The sun setting over the water was making the sky glow with all of these colors I'd never seen before, and, *oh man*, I hadn't packed any paints, only markers and colored pencils, and how would they ever catch colors like that? They wouldn't!

Madeleine slammed on the brakes.

"Doctor, the road ends!"

My mother's hand was tapping her chest again. *Patter, patter, patter.* It was like you could hear her heart beat. "Oh, yes. Well, we're here."

Madeleine frowned. "Here *where*?" Because ahead there were only a gift shop, two shacks, and water. The peninsula had ended.

"*Here*, here. This is the driveway." My mother waved off to the right where a graveled path led into a yard and stopped. Madeleine turned into it.

That's when we saw the house. It wasn't hidden, we'd just missed it because we'd been looking out at the water.

"Mercy," Madeleine said.

I couldn't believe my eyes. This was the house? How could it be? It was small, and my mother did not like small. *I* didn't like small if my mother and me and Madeleine were going to be scrunched up together inside it for three whole weeks. But small seemed right for this house. It seemed perfect. The house looked like a present. Like it had risen up on its little hill just as we'd come around the corner, saying, Here I am—what you've always wanted your house to be. Plain instead of fancy. White wooden boards instead of red bricks. A few funny angles for personality.

I stared at those angles. This must be the back, I decided. It looked as if someone had chopped an upstairs bedroom in half—the roof just ended at its peak, and down came a side wall, straight down to the ground, where it became the side wall of a little sunroom. Odd, very odd. And off of the chopped-up room was an upstairs deck that sat over the sunroom. My heart thumped into my ears when I saw that deck because the chopped-in-half room was *my* room. Nobody told me, I just knew.

I charged out of the car and up the hill like a kid heading straight for his present, and here it was, Christmas!

Madeleine

The glory of Maine, that was what done it. It done it to all of us. Made some old rumble bug of a yearning start up in the pit of our stomachs. Made us search in our inner selves for something grand that could match the sky. But it did it to Homer the worst. When he saw that house sitting plunk on its little hill, looking out at the water, the sun setting behind it, he fell right out of the car and walked up to the door like someone had aholt of his belt and was pulling on it, hard.

"Come back here, Homer Winthrop!" That's me hollering, of course. "Help me unpack this car."

Which I wished I hadn't of done. I wished I'd let him go on being pulled along by the magic.

But I guess he was anyway. There's no stopping magic once't it's begun. What I reckon I ought to be wishing is that we'd had the magic without all the trouble. But maybe you never can.

Never mind. Looking back on it, that trouble did us a whole heap of good.

Plus, it was right entertaining.

3

"*H*omer, you come back here. Help me unpack this car."

Madeleine. Sigh. I turned around and went back to the car.

Madeleine's head was in the trunk. "Give your mother a minute," she muttered.

A minute for what? I looked up at the house. My mother was already going inside. The door was wide open.

"Here," Madeleine said. "Take this." Out of the trunk flew a suitcase. The heaviest one.

I lugged the thing up the hill and onto the porch and on, in through the kitchen (cool, funky, and old), into the living room. Wow. I set down the suitcase and stared. There were views to the harbor out front and to more water out back. The floor was wide wooden boards painted a dark red. The walls were plain and white. It was like being on a ship, that's how the room made you feel. Like it would sway back and forth with the water, but it was sturdy, very sturdy.

Madeleine came up behind me. "Where is she?" she asked in a whisper.

My mother? I shrugged. How would I know?

Madeleine went clunking and banging up the tall, skinny staircase. "Lordy," she said. "These steps is made for shrimps."

I smiled and followed her. It was true. You had to keep your feet turned sideways. Like on a boat, I bet.

Upstairs, my mother was standing in the center of a little hallway, white as a ghost. Four doors opened off the hallway: three bedrooms and one bath.

"Well," Madeleine said, "you point us in what direction."

My mother didn't point. My mother didn't say a word. What was the matter with her, anyhow? Besides the usual, I meant.

"Well." Madeleine went banging on ahead, just as if things were normal. "I'll take this one back here. If ever there's servants quarters, them there's it." And she headed for the chopped-in-half bedroom.

"No!" I hollered. "Stop!" I flung my suitcase in front of her. "That's *my* room!"

This brought my mother to life. "Homer, control yourself. No, it isn't. I'd like you to sleep in this big room on the front. It has a view of the harbor, which you'll appreciate."

"No, I won't. I want the little room on the back." And I took it, just like that.

Nobody said a word. They watched while I flung my suitcase onto the bed and popped up the latches. Uh-oh, wasn't my suitcase. Well, it would do for squatter's rights. I sat down beside it and folded my arms.

"Well, then," Madeleine said in the hallway. "I reckon I'll take this one in the middle."

"Oh, no! Madeleine, *you* take the one in the front. *You* take the one with the view."

"Mercy, no," Madeleine said, and disappeared into the middle one.

My mother was left standing in the hallway. After a minute, I heard her go down the stairs. Madeleine clomped after her. They went out to the car to get more luggage. While they were gone, I carried the suitcase full of my mother's stuff into the room on the front. It *was* a great room. It had a double bed and two big windows looking out at the harbor. Boats floated like black shadows, lights twinkling on their masts. Yep, this was the best bedroom, all right. It was the best room in the house, but I didn't want it.

I went back into my room and looked around. I wanted this one, don't ask me why. It was small, smaller even than my room at school. It had a slanted ceiling and one tiny window that looked smack into the side of the barn next door. In the almost darkness it looked like a closet, but I loved it anyhow. I loved it more than the big room on the front, more than my big old bedroom in Boston that had these fancy bay windows, more than any room I'd ever been in.

I unlatched the door to the deck and stepped outside. My mother and Madeleine were disappearing into the house underneath me.

From the far end, you could look in all directions, even to the harbor out front. I had a view of sailboats, right from my own deck! And there was water out back, too, behind a gift shop and a row of fishing shacks. Those shacks were cool, all rickety and crooked like any second they might fall down. Except that they wouldn't fall down, you could tell. Those were real working shacks. I sighed, feeling happy. Me, Homer Winthrop the Grump!

Back in my room, I turned on a light and flopped down on the bed to take a better look at the place: one picture (a hunting-dog scene), one small desk with a chair, one dresser, one old-fashioned coatrack with hangers, like a closet. Last but not least, the bed I was lying on, tucked under the slant of the ceiling. I could probably have a bad dream and sit up fast and knock myself into a coma. But then who'd have a bad dream in here?

And that's when I saw them—turtles, crawling along my ceiling. Not real ones, of course, but ones someone had painted up there. A row of baby turtles marching along the slope to where two bigger ones waited up on the ceiling. These you saw from the bottom: their brightly patterned undersides, their wrinkled legs, their little toenailed feet. I rose up on my elbows to look. I had turtles up on my ceiling! It was too perfect for words.

"Homer," my mother called from somewhere downstairs. "Come have a bowl of soup. Homer?"

"Coming." I sighed and slowly stood up, but from out in the hallway I turned to look back. The door to the deck was open. Night was creeping in through the screen, sliding around my room. The turtles marched off into darkness.

"Back soon," I whispered, and I swear, my whisper slid out of my mouth and into that room and just sat there, like a promise.

4

In the kitchen, Madeleine and my mother were already eating soup. Madeleine ate hers standing up so she could go on unpacking boxes.

"Madeleine, please!" My mother's eyebrows were dipping. Her bun was restored to its perfect shape. *Doctor* Winthrop was back. "That can all keep till morning. Sit down and rest for a moment. You've had a long day of driving."

"Never you mind me," Madeleine answered as she stomped a carton flat. "I like to eat standing up. That's just the way I am. You can't stop a workhorse from working, and no use tryin'." She took a proud slurp of soup. "You two go on and be on vacation and let me go on being Madeleine. This is my kind of heaven, setting a mess to rights." *Stomp, stomp.* Another carton bit the dust.

My mother couldn't help smiling. "Madeleine on vacation. Ah, well. *Labor omnia vincit.* Work conquers all."

And those were her very words. Now, I mean,

what's quoting some dumb Latin compared to the sight of Madeleine stomping away like a workhorse? My mother is so, well, boring. Boring and predictable. I'd stopped listening to her, because it wouldn't be real words saying anything useful or normal that she was saying. A normal mother would have been talking away right then, explaining about the house, what it was like when we'd been here before. Not my mother. Here's what happened when I asked her a simple question:

"Where did I sleep when I came here before?"

Her eyes got all flitty. The smile fell off her face. "Why...I believe..." She bent over her soup and squinted down into it. "I believe the room you're in now served as the nursery."

The *nursery*. This was the first time I'd ever thought about me as a baby (and I mean how weird is *that*?). I tried to picture a nursery and me in it. Nope, couldn't do it. I couldn't picture me as a baby. Where were my baby pictures?

"Did I sleep with the deck door open? I bet I did." Because I was feeling it in my bones—how fog had rolled in on the baby me and covered me up like a blanket, making me cozy and happy.

My mother stared into her soup bowl as if she'd just seen an ant floating by.

And, dumb me, I went right on talking, letting words roll out of my mouth. "How old was I when I came here? Didn't you worry that I might escape or fall off of the deck?" Which was a silly question. If my mother had told me to stay in bed, I would have stayed in bed. I came into the world obeying my mother. Probably arrived on the very day she requested. January 27—"Hello, in there!" she'd have said, knocking on her belly. "Mozart's birthday. This will do as a day to be born." And then out I came, obedient little Homer Winthrop. "How old was I?" I said now, suddenly hating obedient little Homer. "And who painted those turtles?"

But my mother had turned into an ant-watching statue. As usual, she wasn't going to tell me.

Well, *not* as usual, I wasn't going to give up. The me that hated to talk suddenly wanted to talk her ear off. "Was I a big baby or a little one when we were here?"

My mother opened her mouth. Then she closed it again.

And that was the end of the conversation, if you could even call it that.

I slept with the door to the deck open. Cool night air drifted in through the screen and brushed over my face. Cool night air that was real, not from an air conditioner. No real air made it into my room in Boston. And something else was different. It took me a minute to figure out what it was. There weren't any sounds. None! Only total silence and then the *who-who-o-o*-ing of what must have been a foghorn off in the distance.

The silence didn't make me feel lonely, the way it might have in Boston. It felt sort of alive, as if the ghost of a million Maine nighttimes had come in to curl up in my corner to sleep.

Or the ghost of my own baby self.

"*I* remember you," I said in a whisper. "I don't need any help from my mother."

The trouble was, this was a lie. I didn't remember one thing about the baby Homer. What toys had he liked to play with? What had he liked to eat? When had he said his first word, and what was that word? Didn't know. Couldn't find out. No one was going to tell me.

And I felt my own baby self get angry.

5

I opened my eyes and saw—nothing! Where was I? I sat up and, *bonk!* my head hit the ceiling. Then I remembered, all right. Outside, gulls caw-cawed. A door banged on a fishing shack. I smiled and threw back the covers. Morning in Maine. Morning in a house and a town where my father had been!

Or, morning in mist. Fog had rolled in through the screen. Across the room, the hunting-dog picture came wavering into sight. I yanked on jeans and a T-shirt and threw open my door. The world of the hallway was still out there. Madeleine's room was empty, but my mother's door was closed. I tiptoed to the bathroom. With luck, I could be out in the fog and away, before my mother was even up.

Which was something else new—me going exploring! So what's up with this new you? I asked myself in the mirror. My self didn't know the answer. I didn't *look* any different. Plain brown hair and eyes. Two and a half pimples. Peanuts instead of muscles.

But that was the outside me. Inside, something

different was happening, I could feel it, a kind of rumbling or shuffling or looking for something missing. It was as if the ghost of the baby me had hung out in my room all night looking disappointed. Saying, You know, you're not the kid I expected. I thought you'd turn out to be more exciting. And I had seen right away what he meant. In twelve years of life I'd never had one single adventure worth telling that baby about.

"We're going to change that," I told the kid in the mirror.

The kid smiled back, looking ready to get things rolling. "Okay," he answered.

In the kitchen, Madeleine looked up from scrubbing the oven. "Well, ain't-choo the early bird?"

"Don't say 'ain't,'" I hurried to tell her. "My mother will fire you." It had happened once before. Well, it hadn't just been the "ain't." The woman had said, "I ain't doin' that." But it was the "ain't" that upset my mother the most, I could tell. If she'd said, "I don't care to do that, madam," she might still be collecting her paycheck.

Madeleine pulled her head from the oven. "Homer, if your mother was aiming to fire me for my way of talking, I'd be a dot in your memory by now." The head disappeared again. "Don't you worry, honey." Her voice echoed up from the oven. "We got it worked out between us just fine. Your mother pays no mind to my peculiarities, and I do the same for hers. Which, I might add, is a feat worth bragging on! Have some cereal and fruit. It's all right there on the table."

I sat down and ate. "Where is she, anyway?" I asked. Just to make sure she was where I thought.

"Still asleep, I'm happy to say. Your mother sorely needs this vacation."

It seemed to me it was Madeleine who needed it. I watched the muscles in her back as she scrub, scrub, scrubbed. She was a worker, all right. And pretty cool. My mother had hired her while I was away at school, so I didn't know her all that well yet, but so far I liked what I knew—the way she just told it like it was (which meant she was funny, since the way it usually was was crazy). And the way she made up words to describe things if the one she needed didn't come right to mind, driving my mother nuts. She was sure better than the last few puppets my mother had hired, but still, she *was* a puppet, I had to remember that. The long arm of my mother's law. I didn't blame her, since this was her job. It just meant I had to be fast.

"I'm going out," I whispered to the scrubbing muscles. "Bye now." Then I was out the door, disappearing into the mist before Madeleine could pull her head from the oven and stop me. I couldn't believe I'd done it, but there I was, floating along like a molecule in a cloud, just drifting along being air.

It was busy in Herring Cove, even in the fog. The doors to the shacks out back were open. I could hear a radio playing and the voices of men on the docks and lobster traps rattling, but only once did I see a person—the back of a man bent over working at something, I don't know what, because what could you work at when you couldn't see? Something you knew how to do by heart. On the gift-shop door, invisible hands flipped the sign from "closed" to "open," then the door disappeared. The whole town wavered like my hunting-dog picture. People and buildings rolled in, then rolled off again.

I could paint this fog (or I could have, if I'd brought my paints). I knew just how I would do it, too. I'd use watercolors, letting the wash be the whole painting, but adding in the tip of a boat or two. Or, no, first I would paint in the boats and then do the wash on top of them so that the boats could come floating through. Yes, because fog drifted *over* objects.

I smiled and walked to the general store. Already, traffic was causing problems. A truck towing a boat was blocking the road. *Meep, meep, meep,* said a delivery truck, backing up. "Stop!" somebody yelled. I went inside.

It was a great old store, big and creakity, with wide wooden floorboards and even a wooden ceiling. I stared up at the ceiling. Old, I thought. Which meant something my father had seen. I became hypnotized

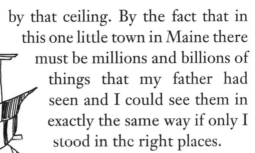

by that ceiling. By the fact that in this one little town in Maine there must be millions and billions of things that my father had seen and I could see them in exactly the same way if only I stood in the right places.

Or asked the right people. I took my eyes off the ceiling. I should find someone who worked here, somebody *old* who worked here, and ask if they'd known my father.

But I knew even while I was looking that I wasn't going to do it. The subject of my father felt private, even scary. That's what living with my mother did to you—turned you into a suitcase brain. Have questions? *Whomp*, throw them in there and slam down the lid. You know, save them, but out of sight. Keep everything out of sight. And don't go around asking questions. You won't get answers. And if you do, you might not like them.

Because why *was* my father a secret? That's what you had to wonder. So, *whomp*. Slam. Lock. Throw away the key.

Wanting to know, but not wanting to, also.

6

"Hey, ouch!" An old man standing at the counter suddenly jumped and spun around, holding his rear end, which a fat rubber band had just hit with a thump, dead center.

A kid with wild red hair popped up from behind the breads and smiled this bright phony smile. "Gee," he said, "pretty good leap for an old man!"

The man shot him a look but limped out of the store without saying a word.

My eyes must have been bugging out of my head or my mouth hanging open. Maybe both, because when the kid saw me looking, his face turned as red as his hair.

"I can explain that," he said.

I doubted this very much.

He came closer and looked around, to see who was looking (no one), then lowered his voice. "See, that old man? Well, he *isn't* old!"

That's funny, he'd looked pretty old to me.

"It's true! I just proved it. Didn't you see him jump? The man's maybe forty. Forty-five, tops."

I *had* seen him jump, but—

"He's wearing a wig and makeup! And he doesn't really limp."

I frowned and pictured the man in my head. I *supposed* that it could be true.

"It *is* true," the kid said, as if he had read my mind. "That man is a hard-core phony baloney. A first-class, card-carrying mysterious person. A one-hundred-percent fake."

"Oh." I stared at the door, wishing the man would come back so I could get another look at him. I'd never seen a hard-core mysterious person before. A *card-carrying* hard-core mysterious person. Well, okay, I'd seen my mother, but she didn't count.

"He's gone," the kid said, seeing me look. "You go out there, he'll be gone, just like that." He snapped his fingers. "That's what's making me crazy. That guy walks around town like he's just a person, but as soon as you try to follow him, he kicks into spy mode. You know, looks behind him to see if you're watching. Won't go home. Then, all of a sudden, when you swear you've been paying attention, he'll just be—" *Snap!* "Gone." The hair bounced on his head.

When you tried to *follow* him?

I guess my thoughts showed on my face because, "You wouldn't?" the kid asked. Not like a criticism, but like he was really and truly curious. "You could see some guy wearing a wig and makeup, and not try to find out why? Not try to solve the mystery?"

I considered all of the mysteries I'd thrown in my suitcase. Yep, I could.

Eyebrows went shooting up. Round coppery-colored eyes stared at me in surprise. "Wow, *I* sure couldn't."

I stared also. Geez. With this kid, you could have a whole conversation and not have to say a word!

"See," he said, "my belief is, when a mystery's right there in front of you, you gotta go out and chase it. You just *have* to, and that's that."

"Oh. It's like a law or something?" I couldn't help smiling.

The kid smiled back. "As a matter of fact, it is. It's the Roger Sweeney Law. Which if you break, you go to prison. Where you get very bored."

I would agree with that. I broke it every day. I was in prison, and I was bored. I guess Homer Winthrop's Law was act like a chicken. Suddenly, I felt a burst of feeling I'd never felt before. Well, I guess I had felt it, but in such teeny little twinges, I couldn't have said it in words. Now I could. The words were: I hate being Homer Winthrop.

"Anyhow, it's not just the wig with this guy. He also uses an alias."

Wow. He did?

The red head nodded. Hair bounced. "He tells people his name is Jack, but just try calling him that. He doesn't even answer. This one time in the store? I heard Martha say, 'Jack? Hey, yo there, Jack.' And he looks at her all blank-like, then he turns red and says, 'Oh, sorry. Hey, you can just call me Buddy. That's what my family does.' Ha! Guess what? He doesn't answer to Buddy, either. And I've never seen him with any family. My guess is he's some kind of a criminal. A big-time criminal. My guess is—"

"Homer Aldrich Winthrop! You get yourself back to that house!"

Uh-oh.

The kid stopped talking. He stared behind me like he was seeing something awesome. Which, of course, he was.

Then he saw Homer Winthrop the Chicken getting dragged right back to prison by a boingy-haired creature in an apron and fluffy slippers.

Look Out Below!

Once upon a time,
there was this kid named
Homer Winthrop.

He came up to Maine
with his mother,
    who looked like this:

And his housekeeper,
who looked like this:

They had no idea what
was about to hit them.

Me, Roger Sweeney,
who looks like this:

After he met me,

Homer Winthrop went from this:

To this:

Except . . .

Whoops.

But do I deserve blame or credit?

Don't know, don't really care.
I'll accept both. Because who wants
to go through life being poultry?

1

"You can let go of me now," I told Madeleine when she'd dragged me across the road. "Where do you think I'm going?"

"Good question!" she answered. "Nowheres, I'd of said if you'd asked me this morning. Nowheres without asking your mother's permission." She did let go of me, but I felt how my shirt still held the knot where she'd twisted it up.

"It's not like I might get lost. This isn't exactly Boston." I wriggled the shirt back into place.

"Which is not the point. You know you have to inform us when you go out. It's just common courtesy. Your mama's been worried."

Here's how worried my mother was: "Morning," she said when we came into the house. Then she opened her paper and started to read.

"Morning," I muttered. I shot Madeleine a look and sat down at the table. My mind was already busy wondering how I would find that kid again. I didn't even know his name. I guessed it was Roger

Sweeney—as in the Law—but I couldn't be sure. It was for sure he knew *my* name. Every person who'd been in that store—every person in a twenty-mile radius!—probably knew my name.

"So," my mother said cheerfully. She put down her paper and smiled at me. Which made me stop wondering and stare at her. My mother was never cheerful. She wasn't even *really* cheerful now. She was being phony cheerful, like someone was holding a gun to her head and saying, You be cheerful, or else.

"So," she repeated. "What are we doing today?"

We? What did she mean by that? This wasn't going to be *that* kind of vacation, was it? The kind where everyone had to do exactly the same thing at exactly the same time? I might as well be at camp! I waited, but she didn't go on. Maybe the "we" had just been that friendly way of talking where the person who says it really means "you." That this really *was* a vacation, and we'd all get to do what we wanted to do and just be friendly about it.

"It'll be cleaning for me," Madeleine answered brightly, as if that's exactly how she'd interpreted it. I am not a "we," her voice was announcing. I rehearsed my own version in my head: It'll be boat-watching for me. Or: It'll be looking for a red-haired kid and spying on fakes for me. I smiled. I guessed I wouldn't say that one.

"I think we should go into Stonehaven," my

mother continued, taking a sip of coffee. "Combine a jaunt with a task I have to accomplish. Perhaps visit a grocery store and buy our meat and poultry."

Well, there went Madeleine, who would have to drive the car. My mother hated driving. One down, one to go. It had all been a setup, my mother's asking what we were doing when she already knew the answer. Classic my mother. Well, this time it wouldn't work.

Madeleine drooped. "Whatever," she muttered gloomily. "You know how I live to jaunt."

My mother smiled in this business-like manner. "You'll like Stonehaven, Madeleine. So will Homer."

I folded my arms. "No I won't. Because I'm not going."

Both of them stared at me. Dumbfounded. This is a word I love. Like people just found their dumbness—meaning dumb in the can't-speak way. Now me, I usually lived in my dumbness. It was words I had to find. But not in Maine. In Maine, I was wordfounded. "I'm going to stay here and watch the boats."

But of course my mother's words came back to her. "Homer…" Her smile wobbled but hung in there. "The boats will be here our entire vacation. They'll be here *this afternoon*. This is only a trip to Stonehaven. I'd like you to come along."

I frowned and folded my arms. "Well, I'd like me to stay here."

We stared at each other awhile. My lips felt sort of dangerous, like they were strangers who might say anything. Like they belonged to that red-haired kid at the store.

"Why?" my mother asked.

"Because," I answered.

She squinted her eyes. I squinted back.

"*Damnum absque iniuria*," she said.

Which I guessed meant that I was going to Stonehaven.

8

Guess what? It was a good thing I did go to Stonehaven. Because two things happened on the way that were very, very important.

The first one was this: We were pulling around the corner, driving slowly up the hill through the fog, when suddenly a face appeared in front of us. Fake Man's face! Madeleine slammed on the brakes, and Fake Man jumped out of the way, and I saw right then that the kid had been right: This was no old man who'd just shot through the air like a bullet!

My mother opened her window to ask if he was all right.

Fake Man's face seemed to hang in the fog. He stared into the car at my mother. My mother stared back. Then she gasped and closed the window. Just like that, *zip!* up shot the window.

"Go on!" she ordered Madeleine. "Go on, just drive away! The man is fine! The man is okay!" This from a woman who despised the word "okay." Who frowned whenever I used it. Her neck shot upward, into its ostrich look.

Madeleine drove away.

Now, what had just happened? I sat there wondering, too stunned to comment. My mother and Fake Man had *known* each other. Which was one pretty strange fact. So strange, my mind couldn't seem to deal with it. There were too many things that it might (or might not!) mean. I threw it in my suitcase brain for thinking about later and stared at the back of my mother's head.

A head that looked like a lightbulb. Or, no, a keyhole, with that bun in its center. Interesting. And where was the key to that head? Nobody knew. Nobody, not even me, her closest—maybe her only!—living relative. That head was just locked up tight as a safe, and the key was missing. No, not missing, *hidden*. Which made me so mad. Which made me madder than mad. Which led to what happened next.

We were driving along the peninsula, nobody talking. Halfway to Stonehaven, the fog disappeared.

"A common phenomenon," my mother informed us, just as if somebody'd asked. Just as if somebody cared. "Herring Cove is farther out in the sea. It's often fogbound when inland is clear. And it can be cooler by ten degrees." She was nervous, saying anything, just to get Fake Man's face out of her window. At least, that's how I was reading it.

I personally refused to be interested. I was interested in the fog we were leaving behind. The fog that had that kid and Fake Man in it. I was interested in why my mother could give orders in Latin, a language nobody understood, and have people always obey them. I was interested in how her whole life was one big fat secret, starting with my father, and nobody made her explain things.

Had anyone asked "Who was that man back there whose nose you just closed in the window?" No, no one had asked.

"What's the task?" I demanded suddenly. "In Stonehaven. What's the thing you have to accomplish?"

No answer.

"What—is—the—task?" My voice kicked at her seat like a foot, surprising all of us, me especially. I didn't even know voices could kick. I didn't even know I wanted to ask this question. Maybe I didn't. I just needed to ask something.

Still no answer. Madeleine stole a peek at my mother, whose head wasn't moving. My bet was her eyes were popping and her brain was whirling, wondering, Where has my meek little son gone? Where is Homer Aldrich Winthrop, who always does what he's told?

"What—is—it?" I demanded. Kick, kick, kick. Kicking felt good. Homer Aldrich had never known that, the dumb puppy-dog moron.

And you know what? Kicking worked. My mother went sort of limp. Her neck got shorter. Then she simply told me the truth. She said, "It's a matter regarding the house. I'm listing it with a real estate agent."

I couldn't believe my ears. "You mean you're *selling* it?" It couldn't be! I'd only just found the house, and now she was going to sell it? And if I hadn't happened to ask, she'd have sold it without telling me?

My mother sighed. "Yes, Homer. A second home is a burden, especially when you don't use it. You need caretakers. Gardeners. People to rent it."

"Then don't rent it. We'll use it! I'd come up here every year. I'd come *happily*! I love it in Maine! I love that house. That *particular* house."

This must have shocked her. I know it shocked me. Me, Old Picklepuss as Madeleine called me, showing all that excitement. *Feeling* all that excitement.

"Homer..." Her voice was getting quivery. "It's a lot more involved than you know. You simply must trust me on this."

"Well, that's too bad, 'cause I don't. You can give me the house. *I'll* take care of it."

Which, okay, was pretty funny. I gave my mother and Madeleine credit—they didn't laugh.

My mother didn't say a word after that, except to croak out directions. She didn't say a word all the way into Stonehaven. Didn't say a word as we passed through the main part of town, straight on to the grocery store, where we bought what we needed, then back through Stonehaven again. Now I *wanted* to stop. This looked like a town from the olden days, the kind with buildings that might not have changed since my father had seen them. The kind that might sell paints. That *would* sell paints, because I'd seen galleries wherever I looked on Main Street. But now, of course, we wouldn't. My mother was not even turning her head to look out the window.

What had she meant by "a lot more involved than you know"? Involved how? Because of my father? Because of Fake Man? Because of...what? It was like the lid to my suitcase kept wiggling open, then slamming shut, showing me peeks of a mystery. Showing me that maybe, inside of my own head, there were answers if I could only reach in and grab them fast.

"Hey," Madeleine said suddenly. "I think we forgot the jaunt part." She'd made the turn onto the peninsula.

My mother sighed, loudly. "I hadn't noticed a prevailing spirit of jauntiness."

I made a face at the back of her head. A jaunty face.

"What about the real estate agent's office?" Madeleine asked.

Doesn't matter, I wanted to say. Because we're not selling the house. But I kept my mouth shut. I wanted to hear what my mother would answer. From here on out, I would study her every move. Observe her weak spots. Find the key to that locked-up head.

"We'll have to postpone that," she answered. The head fell back on the headrest. "One of my headaches is coming on."

"Oh, mercy, no." Madeleine clicked her tongue.

I clicked mine also. This was perfect, just perfect. It was our life's story: Whenever real information leaked out of my mother, along came one of her headaches, guaranteed foolproof to plug her back up.

Madeleine patted my mother's arm. "Well, let's hope it won't be a bad one." But it would be, I could tell. The head had started to droop, the neck was caving in.

I closed my eyes and stared at the back of my eyelids. There went my mother, the long-necked ostrich. Now she looked more like a duck, her face falling forward, flattened by the headache. I could see Duck Face without even looking. It was the face of my mother leaving—wilting, wilting, *gone*. She would follow her duck bill into the house. She would follow it up the stairs to her bed. Not that it mattered, of course. My mother was never there, even when she was there. She lived somewhere off in her head, dropping in just to give orders.

Before I knew I was going to do it, I pictured an arrow shot into the back of that head. I stared at it in alarm. Who had shot that arrow?

"I did," I whispered, my heart starting to race. But I hadn't meant it, not in the way it looked. I opened my eyes and stared at my mother's head, which was reassuringly arrowless. "I hope you feel better soon," I told her. "I hope that it's not a bad one."

"Thank you, Homer," she said. She leaned back against the seat. "I hope so also."

9

By the time we got back from Stonehaven, the fog was history. The boats were moving, in and out of the harbor.

I headed straight for the docks.

"You come back here and eat some lunch," Madeleine called after me.

I came back.

Madeleine fixed me a tuna-fish sandwich, then went upstairs to check on my mother, who'd wandered away like a ghost.

A ghost who knew Fake Man, I thought as I chewed. A ghost Fake Man knew. And the feeling was sort of haunting, like I couldn't quite grab on to it. Wait till I told that kid! Wait till he heard how his card-carrying mysterious person was connected to mine! But the idea of telling it didn't really feel real. *Feeling* it didn't feel real. Your own mother shouldn't be a card-carrying mysterious person. Somebody you didn't even know. Somebody who'd maybe had a life you hadn't even guessed about.

Madeleine came back downstairs and sank into a seat across from me. "This one's a humdinger," she said.

That meant three days, maybe four. Probably lots of vomiting. I made myself take a bite of my sandwich. I made myself chew.

"I wonder," Madeleine said thoughtfully. She was staring up at the curtains, not really seeing them.

I waited. I managed another bite. "You wonder what?" I finally asked.

Madeleine looked at me in surprise, like she'd forgotten that I was there. I swear, sometimes grown-ups live on another planet, even the cool ones like Madeleine. "Well, I wonder about your mama—was she ever different?"

Her question shocked me, it was so like what I'd been thinking. I put down my sandwich and stared. Could *everyone* read my mind?

Madeleine stared back. "You know what I mean? With your father and all, back then."

Well, I hadn't exactly meant that, but I caught her drift. My father *had* married her. There must have been something about her to like.

"I bet she was." Madeleine was squinting at the curtains again. "I bet she used to be happy. I bet losing your daddy's what changed her. You can tell she just loved him to pieces."

"*What?* She won't even *talk* about my father! She keeps his pictures turned upside down in a drawer!"

"Which is exactly what I'm getting at. You can see how it hurts her to talk. And it's not hard to guess. Imagine, two fancy brains like those, having each other to talk to. And him such a handsome man. I've seen those pictures." Madeleine shook her head. "It must have been quite a life before he got sick. I bet no one could ever replace him."

And just what did she mean by *that*? I pushed back my chair and stood up. "I'll be out on the docks," I told her, and left.

My mother still had me. Didn't that count for something?

I wandered around. Hung out at the general store. No sign of red hair. The place was hopping, though. The whole town must buy their lunch in the store and eat it out on the deck. But it wasn't people from town, I saw when I'd watched for a while. It was tourists, some coming in the front door, some coming in the back. The ones coming in the back had arrived on boats and had come clanking up the boat ramp.

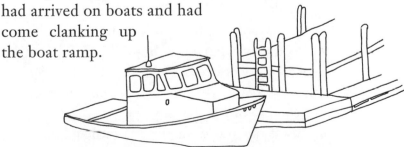

There were boats of all shapes and sizes tied up at the floating docks, and more tied up out in the water. Working boats to the right, playing boats to the left, that seemed to be the system. People from the boats out in the water came rowing or *putt-putt*ing into shore in smaller ones. People in, people out, people in. Dogs, kids, groceries, building supplies, all of it going somewhere in boats. Man, I thought, they need some traffic signals out there. I tried to guess which big boat the people in the smaller boats were headed for. Usually I was right. People looked like their boats, I decided.

If I had a boat, what kind would I want it to be? I didn't even know. I couldn't picture me in a boat. I stared down at the boats tied up at the public landing. Maybe one of those small ones that you could row. Yes, that green one. But while I was looking, the little green boat stopped being a boat and became a floating triangle. A triangle divided in half by a shadow— dark on one side, light on the other. Which meant the colors changed at that point: dark green turning into yellow. Really, the colors were exactly the same on both sides if you wanted to get technical, if you wanted to go by what your brain *knew* and not by what your eyes were seeing. Which I didn't. I liked how my eyes really saw things and how my fingers always itched to draw what my eyes saw.

But it was one more way I was weird and different

from other people, I knew that. Anybody else standing on this dock would be looking at that boat and thinking: *Water! Fun! Exploring!* I'd never met another person on the whole earth who saw things the way that I did. Who felt sort of, well, *hungry* to pass things in through their eyeballs and out again, onto paper. Who—

But my triangle was turning back into a boat. A man and a boy had climbed down into it. While I watched, they untied and pushed away from the dock. The man sat in the end of the boat, his face turned up to the sun, letting the kid do all the rowing. That kid was his son, I bet. You could see how the father trusted him. He did a good job, too, guiding the boat past the other boats, past the end of the pier. They were headed for an island. What would they do when they got there? I wondered. And suddenly, more than anything, I really wanted to know that.

What a man and his son would do.

10

I was still standing there watching that little boat when, *eeech!* a bike screeched to a halt beside me.

It was the red-haired kid, looking glad to see me. "Hey, cool, you survived!"

I couldn't help smiling. "Sure." And I shrugged, as if being dragged home by the T-shirt was nothing, really. A minor inconvenience. Which, with Madeleine, it sort of was.

"Roger Sweeney. Pleased to meet ya." He held out his hand for me to shake.

I'd never met anyone my own age who shook hands, but I shook his, gladly. "Homer Winthrop. But I guess you know that already." I felt a blush start to creep up my neck.

Roger snorted. "So was that your *mother*?"

"No! That was Madeleine. Our housekeeper. And driver. And cook. And general dragger-home-er."

"Your Homer dragger-home-er!"

I smiled. "Yeah, when she can find me. Which in

Boston is not so easy." Now, why had I said that? I had never once, not *ever* (until that morning), hidden from Madeleine. Hadn't even tried to.

"Boston." Roger looked thoughtful. "So you're here on vacation. I thought so. You ever been here before?"

"No." Which wasn't exactly true, although in a way it was.

Roger squinted. "You know," he said, "that might just be useful."

I blinked. "Useful?"

"Yeah. Nobody knows you, you know? You can go where I can't go. Do what I can't do."

Uh-oh. No, I couldn't.

"You know that man back in the store?"

I nodded. "Fake Man," I managed to say.

Roger smiled. "Yeah, cool, Fake Man. Do you think he saw you with me?"

Something told me I should say yes, but it told me a second too late. "Well," I said, "not probably."

"Great! That guy is up to something, and I plan to find out what."

I hoped that my face looked normal, that it wasn't showing what I was thinking, which was, Me be useful? No way in a million years! "What do you think he's up to? How are you going to find out?"

"I'm going to see where he lives for starters. And I want to know what he does on Owl Island. Every single day, he gets on the ten-thirty boat wearing that lame disguise. I can't believe people buy it."

"I bought it," I admitted. "If you don't look at him all that closely, he just looks a little bit strange."

"Well," Roger said. "Maybe. I guess it looks lame to me because the first time I saw him he wasn't wearing it. And he wasn't limping. He was coming out of the woods up by the lighthouse looking perfectly normal. Carrying something in front of him, all wrapped up in plastic. I noticed him because he seemed so surprised when he saw me. Sort of sneaky or guilty."

"How did you know it was him? I mean if he wasn't wearing the wig..."

"The shoes," Roger said. "Those dumpy old Reeboks with the yellow laces. When he went by, I noticed them right away because—" He stopped and held up a foot to show me his own yellow laces. "I'm a yellow fanatic. I just can't help it. I know, *dork*, you can say it." He shrugged and put down his foot.

I wasn't thinking dork. I was thinking, Wow, I'd like to draw those feet! Those clunky old worn-out shoes with their sparkling new yellow laces—fresh icing on a dirty old cake. I was thinking I'd like to *be* a person who might be useful.

"Anyhow, the next day, I'm watching people get on the boat to Owl Island, the *Emily Ann*, and those same feet go by. The same feet on the same legs, except that the legs aren't moving so fast. When I look up, there's an old man's head on top of the body. Except that it isn't really. I know right away it's only a wig and sunglasses and a bad makeup job. Really, it *isn't* a good disguise. The makeup's all caked. The wart moves around. But you're right. You have to be paying attention. I hate that, how nobody really sees things."

I was hypnotized. Spellbound, I guess you'd call it. By a Roger who really *saw* things, but in a much different way from me. By a Roger who let the hair grow wild on his head. Who wore those yellow laces. Who thought he was a dork and didn't mind that. By the fact that when *he* found a card-carrying mysterious person he didn't sit around and feel haunted, he sprang into action like a firecracker that had been lit.

"So," Roger went on, "I start watching. Every day this guy takes the *Emily Ann* out in the morning and comes home on the four-thirty boat and he's always carrying a cardboard carton. I decide to follow to see where he lives. But he won't go home. At least not when I'm watching. He knows that I'm there. He knows I'm wise to him. So he wanders around, going nowhere, lugging that big old carton, which can't be easy. Now, Homer, what does that tell you?"

My eyes were popping, I felt it. "That the man has something to hide."

"Bingo," Roger answered. "And it must be something important if he has to wear a disguise. And what's in that carton, you've got to wonder. Why won't he set it down? My guess is he's smuggling something."

My lips didn't move, but my eyes must have said, *Smuggling?* because "Why not?" Roger replied. "Hey, there's a black market for everything. Those are rare and endangered plants out on that island. Some only grow there and over in Scotland. That man could be digging them up and selling them. Or maybe he's found some kind of buried treasure. There've been hundreds of wrecks out there. That would *really* be cool. Or it could be—" Suddenly, he stopped talking and looked straight into my eyes. His face turned red. My eyes hadn't said a word, I swear it! I'd just been listening and thinking, Wow, smuggling! "Okay, I admit it," he sighed. "It's probably something a lot more boring. Like maybe he's selling drugs."

Selling drugs? Boring? Now my eyes *were* talking.

"By boring I mean ordinary. More realistic. My imagination gets carried away sometimes. Well, all of the time, actually. Which I don't mind, but I know other people do."

"*I* don't," I told him. And I didn't. I admired his imagination. I knew exactly how I would draw it. I'd make it big and round, like a bubble over his head, full of stars and faraway mountains and exclamation points. I'd put one little blip of sunlight on the outside of the bubble.

Roger smiled. "Really? Cool. Hey, you want to come back to my house?"

Did I ever!

But suddenly, I pictured that bubble popping. I saw how it could float you anywhere and then, *bang*, drop you to earth.

"Can't," I answered. And I put a hand over my mouth to stop Homer the Chicken from clucking.

11

At home, Madeleine was running up and down the stairs, being slave labor.

I flung myself down on the sofa and scowled up at the ceiling in the general direction of my mother's bedroom. Whatever Madeleine was being paid, it couldn't possibly be enough. One of these days, she'd quit. Which, I'm ashamed to say, brought me a tingle of satisfaction, since I was currently mad at both of them.

I was also mad at myself. I couldn't believe I'd turned down a chance to see Roger's house. Not that turning it down was stupid. That invitation was not just a simple thing. Saying yes would be saying yes to a spying-on-Fake-Man partnership. And oh, sure, maybe the new me *wanted* to be Roger's partner, but maybe he wasn't quite ready yet. I mean, he'd only been born for one day.

So, in a way, I'd been smart to say no. Except that I hadn't only said no. I'd also said, "I'll come tomorrow." Which is classic Homer Aldrich Winthrop.

Don't get yourself out of a problem, just give yourself time to worry.

Not only that, but I'd added, "I'm too busy today." And since I wasn't busy, it meant I had to come here—back to the house of Duck Face and Madeleine—and stay here the rest of the day. Double-dip classic Homer Winthrop.

"Lordy, lordy," I heard Madeleine mumbling somewhere upstairs. And she added a sigh you could hear from the sofa. Yep, she was reaching her limit, all right.

I closed my eyes and pictured how the ending would probably happen. Madeleine would throw down her shiny apron—no, she'd take that with her—she'd bounce a bowl off the kitchen table and (after stopping to clean up the mess) tell my mother to go fly a kite. Or something more unusual, which I hoped I would be there to hear.

"Homer?"

I jumped and nearly fell off the sofa. When I opened my eyes, Madeleine was looking down at me.

"Yeah?" I closed my eyes again.

"I just wanted to say I'm sorry. I owe you an apol-er-gee."

I didn't answer. An apol-er-gee? What was that, some kind of spacecraft?

"I shouldn't have yelled at you out in public this morning. It was a very rude thing to do."

I sighed and sat up. "Oh, that's okay." It wasn't, but I forgave her. I would always forgive Madeleine. I'd hate it if she really quit.

"Seems like some days you wake up and your knickers are all in a twist. And that sets you to walking crooked, you know?"

I frowned. What in the world were knickers? Were we talking *underpants* here?

"So then off you go, and the first thing you know you've hit a wall. Walked smack into it. And of course you blame the wall. Shouldn'ta been there in front of you!"

I knew that feeling. But today I guessed I had been the wall.

I stared down at the braided rug and analyzed its colors. (Pink weaving into green weaving into blue into purple. I'd get that pink out of there. Change it to yellow.) "Well, maybe sometimes it *is* the wall's fault," I answered. "And maybe the wall even knows it. I mean if the wall was acting stupid or something." Why *had* I gone out without telling her? Madeleine wouldn't have stopped me. I'd been making some kind of a point. Showing off for the baby me.

Madeleine chuckled. "Nah. I've talked to a lot of walls. Not a one of 'em stupid."

*   *   *

At dinnertime, Madeleine fixed me some chicken and sat at the table while I ate it.

"So," she said, "what did you find to do with yourself out there?"

Now, as you know, this is a tricky question. "Nothing" is never a good enough answer, even when it's true, which today it definitely wasn't. Madeleine had already seen me with Roger.

"Well . . ." I took a bite of potato. "I met this really cool kid, the one you saw this morning? I think he lives here all year round."

"Well good for you, Homer." She helped herself to a drumstick off my plate. "I'm glad you found you somebody." The eyebrows suddenly dipped. "Your mother's not going to be much use to you for a while."

I didn't comment. Since when had she been any use? But I knew what Madeleine wanted. I was supposed to ask, How's she feeling? Well, I wouldn't. Because really, I didn't care.

"Well, then." Madeleine cleared her throat. "Tell me this new friend's vitals: name, address, barber shop's telephone number." She held up her foot in its fuzzy slipper. "I reckon I finally found me the person to trim these ugly feet."

I stared at the slipper. It looked exactly like Roger's head, except in blue! I started laughing, I couldn't help it. I laughed and laughed. Not laughing at Roger but because a head could look like a slipper.

Or no, because a slipper could look like a head. Or no, because of this person who noticed the two relating. Ahh, Madeleine, she was cool, all right. I wished *she* were my mother. If Madeleine got sick, I would care.

Apol-er-gee accepted.

12

The next morning, I stared through the door to the deck. The sky was a pure and perfect blue. The few fluffs of clouds looked pasted on, like in one of those pictures where you could pick up the objects and move them around and they'd stick anywhere. If this were a picture like that, here was how I'd arrange things: I'd move that lobster shack to the right (so you could see the docks behind it). I'd stack those lobster traps higher (make the pile impressive). I'd, yikes! bring back all of the water! Wow, this must be low tide, but *really*, the whole cove was empty. The boats tied up at the docks rested on mud and rocks with no water in sight.

I hurried downstairs, anxious to *be* in a day this blue, and to check out the tides. Anxious to hook up with Roger. Who cared about Fake Man? If I had to follow him, I could and I would, that's how I felt at that moment. Like anything was possible.

My mother had made it down to the table, but she didn't look good. Her eyes were sunken into her head and had dark shadows around them, as if someone had come in and punched her during the night.

"Hey, did you check out the cove?" I said, to make conversation, feeling generous in my good mood. "Somebody pulled the plug!"

My mother managed a smile. "Low tide," she said. I could see how talking hurt her, but she was doing it anyway. She was being generous, too. "There's a twelve-foot variance in tides," she explained. "Dramatic, isn't it?"

Madeleine set a grapefruit down in front of me. "Eggs?" she asked. She rapped on the top of my head. "Cereal? Muffin?"

"No. Brains, I think." I smiled. "Though there might be some eggs over here." I tapped behind my ear.

Madeleine rolled her eyes. "Okay, Mr. Wiseguy. And for breakfast you'd like . . . ?"

"Hmm. I'd say French toast. Blueberry waffles. Maybe a pancake or two." I glanced at my mother to see whether she found my jokes funny or annoying. Neither, of course, since she had gone back to her usual nonlistening self.

Madeleine's eyes whirled. "Oh, sure. Coming right up. But you better have you some cereal to eat while you wait. You might get hungry." She poured granola into a bowl and plopped it down in front of me. "So, what are you up to today? Plans with your new friend?"

And like lightning, my mother was back, hearing everything. "Friend? What new friend?"

Then the new Homer Winthrop did something the old one would never have dared to do. He ignored her. "No plans," I told Madeleine, not mentioning going to Roger's house in case someone decided to stop me. "We're going to just, you know, hang out on the docks and stuff—I mean, and so forth" (the word "stuff" not being allowed in my mother's ears).

My mother was staring at me like I'd just dropped in from some other planet. Which I guess in a way I had. I smiled and bent over my cereal. Looking for ants. Let's see how *she* liked being ignored.

She didn't like it one bit. Her eyes bored holes in the top of my head. "Homer? Who is this new friend?"

"Just a kid—I mean, person." Using her own technique: Say the basics but leave out the major details. "Roger Sweeney."

The eyes went on boring. I went on smiling and slurping up cereal.

"Homer!" Now this voice was hard to ignore. "I'd prefer us to keep to ourselves. I don't want you making connections. Announcing that we're here."

My spoon stopped on its way to my mouth. My eyes bugged into the next state. *Announcing* that we were here? All I'd done was make one friend! Or *start* to make one friend. I hadn't even done that yet.

"And why not?" I demanded.

My mother's eyes sank back into their shadows.

"Homer, please," she said quietly. "It's a simple request. I'd like you to honor it." Which back in Boston might have worked. Here it wouldn't.

"No, it isn't! It isn't simple at all! You have to tell me *why*."

My mother sighed, and her sigh was so loud and so real and so shaky I was almost sorry I asked. Almost but not quite.

"*Tell* me. *Why* can't I make connections?"

We stared at each other.

"Because I came here to tend to my business, not to revisit the past. I don't want to deal with visitors. Is that too much to ask? Now, please, no more questions."

No more questions? Ha! To the new Homer Winthrop, those were fighting words.

Madeleine

See, now in my opinion, she done handled everything wrong. Dr. Winthrop, I mean. She was never honest with Homer. She had so many chances to just say things right out, and she never took nary a one of them.

Well, I guess that's because she wasn't saying them to herself. I remember this one particular morning. I was standing there looking out of the window, seeing the water all shiny and bright, seeing the clouds racing through the sky, seeing a boat setting out to sea like the moon sailing into tomorrow, and I thought to myself, Jiminy Cricket! Every last person in this whole blamed beautiful world ought to stand up and jump for joy and be happy, no questions asked.

But what did I see when I went in the kitchen? I saw Dr. Winthrop sitting at the table, all locked up inside of herself. I saw her Gloomy Gus of a son coming into the room finally looking happy because he'd made him a friend and had a day to look forward to. And then danged if his mother didn't snap up that happiness like she was a frog sitting on a lily pad and the happiness was a gnat just happening by.

"Don't go making connections," that's what she said to her son. Imagine, just when he'd finally found him a friend. And "I came here to tend to my business, not to revisit the past." Which was just plain ole nonsense from start to finish, that past being what it was. Mercy, you can't sit on a bomb like that one and expect it to not blow up.

Well, there's folks who's just like that, I guess— who can't look their feelings square in the face, who for sure won't talk about them till they're made to—and Homer might have grown up being one of them, if things hadn't happened the way they did. Old Picklepuss was more like his mama pickle than he'd have cared to know about.

It's right interesting, I believe, what gives a body his shape. You can't really say how a young person's gonna turn out. Some folks get sit on, it squashes them flat. Others just bite the ole butt what's sitting on them, and lickety-split, they're outta there. Homer, I believe, could have gone either way.

I think it was Maine made him go how he did.

I know it was Maine made me go how I did. I watched Homer sit at that table and stare at the top of his mother's head, not saying a word. I felt rebellion brewing, I have to confess it. I thought to myself, Homer Winthrop will soon be biting the butts what are sitting on him. And do you know what? I didn't make one move to stop it.

In fact, I did worse than that. I fed the rebellion outright. "Homer," I said when his mother had gone back upstairs. "You and Roger go on and have you some fun. Just check in with me now and again. Let's say every three hours. And dinner's at six-thirty." Lordy, can you believe it?

Well, I reckon I couldn't help it. I'd seen a sailboat sailing into tomorrow. Had me a taste of joy.

13

Roger's house backed right up to the cove. His yard went down to the water, where there was even a little dock. I loved the place the minute I saw it. You could tell a real family lived there, and lived there year-round.

"Ignore the mess," Roger said when we went inside. "But be careful. You can get lost in this place. I have an uncle who's in here somewhere. And I think maybe a dog, too."

The mess was impressive. But when you looked at it more closely, you saw that it *wasn't* a mess. The house wasn't dirty at all, it was just very, very full. There were knickknacks, photographs, knitting yarn, gardening tools, bunches of flowers stuck in jars (most of the flowers wilted), mail order catalogs, magazines, books, books, and more books. But all of it orderly. All of it clean. All of it interesting. I loved the feeling that the people who lived in this place had a life—a *real* life, where they cared about things and probably had conversations about which of those things mattered most. I felt so jealous it hurt. I had a pain, right in the pit of my stomach.

"My mom's the town librarian," Roger announced. "In case you couldn't tell. And my dad's a writer. Except that right now he's a writer who also builds houses because books-to-be don't pay any bills."

"Wow. You're so lucky." So it was true, all those conversations.

Roger frowned and looked around, as if he was searching for that luck. "Well, maybe. You live in Boston, right?"

"Yes."

"Suburbs or city?"

"City."

"Really? Where? Me and my dad go down to Boston a lot. He grew up in Massachusetts. We go to Red Sox games."

I had never once been to a Red Sox game. I'd never—

"Homer? So where do you live? Right in the *city* city?"

I nodded. "On Beacon Hill. When I'm not away at school. Which I usually am." I could see by his face that he knew what those facts meant. They meant money, as if it mattered. As if I wouldn't trade my house for Roger's in one second.

"Oh." His eyes wandered away. After a minute, he said, "Your father still down there?" his voice sounding all flat and neutral like he didn't really care but thought he would just ask this. I knew what he was doing. He was fishing to hear what a father did who could make us all of that money.

I shook my head.

"Divorced?"

"Nope. Dead."

I hated the part that came next. Roger would get embarrassed and blink at me once with pity and then look away. He would say, "Oh. Sorry," and worry that he should say more. But *what* more? he'd be wondering, so he wouldn't say anything.

"Oh," Roger said. "Sorry." He blushed, blinked at me once, and looked away.

"It's okay." I shrugged. I hated this next part, too. "My father died when I was a baby. Can't miss what you never had, right?" Wrong. As if a father could die and not matter as long as you hadn't *known* him. It was dumb, but it worked every time: people nodded and went on to the next subject, looking relieved.

"Well, I don't know about that." Roger frowned and looked at me. "I bet you miss not having a father. I bet you miss him a lot. I bet you wish you had him. Right?"

I just stood there, shocked. No one had ever said this to me. Not once. "Yes," I finally answered, but the word came out a croak, so I said it again, louder. "Yes. I do. I miss him a lot."

"Man. That's really sad. How did your father die?"

I shrugged, out of the habit of shrugging, then wished I could take it back. Shrugs were for when something didn't matter. This mattered, and Roger knew it. "A neurological illness. That's all I know. My mother, well, she doesn't talk much. Especially about my father."

"Really? How come?"

Whew. How come. "I don't know exactly. My mother is just, well, she's not even like a mother. She's more like a machine." And how could you love a machine? You couldn't. "She's like this sad, mopey machine who, well, you don't even know what she's feeling. Or *if* she's feeling. She doesn't talk *with* you, she just talks *at* you. You know, drops by just to give orders." Orders such as, Don't go making connections. Well, I was happy to say, here I was making some, big-time!

Roger looked thoughtful. "If she's sad, then she's feeling *that*."

"Hmm, maybe. But if she is, then it's *all* she's feeling. And she's not going to talk about it. Which means whatever she says is a kind of pretending." Wow. I hadn't even known I had known that. "She's an act. She's like a robot mother. And our house in Boston is like a museum, not a place where somebody lives. And she sends me to a boarding school in Connecticut, where my roommate hates me." Now, where had those words just come from? They'd marched themselves up and out of my mouth like little people with minds of their own. "And I almost never go home. I'm at camp for most of the summer. Not that it matters because why should I go home? The robot doesn't notice I'm there."

"Gee," Roger said. "That's awful." He looked around the room with a whole new look on his face like now he had found his luck.

14

Roger's bedroom was a true mess, the kind where you really could lose a dog or an uncle.

"Whoa," I said, impressed.

"Yeah," Roger answered.

I thought of what my mother and Madeleine said when I dropped one little thing on the floor.

"My mom won't come in here," Roger told me. "She says if I want to live like an animal, that's my business. Then she oinks and slams the door. Sometimes she oinks for the whole morning if she gets a good look."

Roger shook the blanket crumpled up on his bed. Stuff tumbled and rolled and crashed onto the floor, then he spread the blanket out flat so we could sit on the edge of the bed. "There," he said, sounding a little surprised that the trick had worked. He'd created a neat flat space. "Hey, sheets!" he said. "How did they get on here?"

I wanted a bed like this one. *I* wanted to live like

an animal. Well, okay, probably I really didn't, but I would like to try it, just for fun.

When we sat down on the cleared space, Roger suddenly got serious. He looked me right in the face. "Okay," he said. "Here's the plan about Fake Man. Tonight, when he gets off the *Emily Ann*? You're going to follow him. Find out where he lives."

I was?

"You can do that, right?"

I looked away. "Sure. I can." I *could* do it. I would. I would do anything Roger wanted. He was the first real friend I'd ever had.

"Great! Hey, you want to go see the lighthouse? Have you been there yet?"

I shook my head. "No. I mean, no I haven't, but yes I'd like to." I smiled, and we raced to the door, trampling stuff all the way.

The lighthouse was the best thing I'd seen in Herring Cove. The house part was now a museum, but the light still worked. It actually guided boats.

"Wow," I said, but wow didn't begin to touch it.

"Cool, huh?" Roger jumped down to the rocky beach and skipped a rock over the water. I skipped one also. "Just watch you don't hit that cormorant," Roger said.

My hand stopped in midair.

A black bird suddenly popped up from under the water out by the lighthouse. "See?" Roger said. "Now watch him, he'll disappear." The minute he said it, the bird dove under. "Let's guess where he's coming back up." We both guessed, and we both were wrong.

"Those birds are so cool. They're like these little animal submarines. If I was the enemy, I'd wire them up and train them, make them my mini periscopes. Sometimes you see seals out here, too. And you'll see guillemots if you go sailing. My dad once saw a river otter up by the woods, but that's a pretty unusual thing."

"Did you ever see a moose?"

"Did I ever! This one time, we're coming home from the airport? *Smash*, we plow right into one with our car. Man, it was good-bye Honda! It was a miracle we weren't killed. That moose's antlers were as big as my body. One of them crashed in through the windshield. The moose wasn't dead, though. He just sort of huffed himself off the hood of our car and took off into the woods, not really running but just moving moose-like. I hope he didn't die later. I hate it when animals die. There was this great little dog named Nellie that sort of belonged to the lighthouse because her owner wrote a book about her and called her the lighthouse dog. She died from old age, but still, it was sad, you know? Now he has Good Golly Miss Molly, who looks just like her. She's cool too. Now there's a book about her, so *she's* the lighthouse dog."

I was breathless just listening. And happy. I have to say, I hadn't once, since we got to the lighthouse, thought about Fake Man.

But then we went into the lighthouse museum. The very first thing we saw was this quilt hanging on the wall. It had the boats of Herring Cove stitched into its squares.

"That's my uncle Doug's lobster boat," Roger said, pointing to a square. "And my friend Norm's sailboat. And here's the *Sarah Blue*. It's the mail boat to Owl Island. That's all there was, back before the captain had the *Emily Ann* built. That's how you *had* to go out to the island. You still can if you want to." I stared at the *Sarah Blue*, and I swear, the little face stitched in the window looked just like Fake Man's. *Spy! Spy!* he hissed down from the wall.

After that, I did not see one thing. Or yes, I did.

I looked into the glass display cases, and I saw my own face— the face of the kid who'd be following Fake Man. And that face looked scared. That face was saying to me, Who do you think you're fooling? You're not the *real* Homer Winthrop. The real Homer Winthrop is too big a coward to be a spy!

"I better go home," I told Roger suddenly. We were walking back to his house. "My mother and I—we're busy this afternoon."

I could tell Roger didn't believe me. He gave me a look but didn't comment. We walked along for a while without talking.

"Homer," he said finally, "you don't have to follow Fake Man if you don't want to. I won't get mad."

I stopped walking. Man, I loved how he could do that—could read my mind—even if what he was reading was embarrassing.

But he'd only read part of it. Because part of me *did* want to do it. It wanted to more than anything. And that part hated that Roger thought I didn't. "But I *do* want to," I said. "I do and I will!"

Roger still looked like he didn't believe me, but he shrugged and started us walking again. "Well, okay. If you really want to. But you don't have to do it in this serious-like way. Do it in a not-really-following way. You know? Just sort of wander around, just sort of see where his house is. So he won't even know you're there."

I nodded. I could just sort of wander around. Just sort of see where his house is. That made it sound easy. Like not really spying at all.

"Then, as soon as you find out, come over to my—oh, shoot, I have to go out tonight. Okay, look. Call and leave a message on our machine. If you found out where Fake Man lives, say, 'Hi, Roger, this is William. Talk to you later.' If you didn't, you say, 'Hi, Roger, this is Homer. Talk to you later.' Got it? If you fail, you're yourself."

I couldn't help laughing. "Well, gee, thanks a lot."

Roger looked embarrassed, but only for one second, because his bubbling, planning, solve-every-mystery self just went right on rolling along. "Sorry, didn't mean it like that! Anyhow, you won't fail. So then tomorrow, at ten-thirty, you'll go make sure Fake Man gets on that boat. As soon as he does, come straight to my house. Because while Fake Man is out on the sea, we'll check out his house. See what the man is up to. See if you need to follow him onto that boat or not."

See if I needed to follow him onto that boat?

Or not!

15

"You're looking glum, chum." Madeleine had come into my bedroom to run a mop under my bed, never mind that I was lying on top of it.

"Nah, I'm not." And I wasn't really. Glum wasn't exactly the word. Nervous, that was the word. I was also bored with being inside, but I couldn't say this to Madeleine who'd say, "Well, then why don't you go outside?" Because what could I answer to that, "I can't, because of this lie I just told Roger"?

When Madeleine left, I stared at the turtles for a while. I thought how they were a lot like me. If something scared them, they pulled their heads into their shells and stayed very still. That was me, all right. The me who didn't want to follow Fake Man. Who didn't want to lead Roger back to his house (to do *what*, exactly?) if I actually found it. The me who was definitely *not* going out to some island. The me who wanted to just sit there, inside my shell, hiding from any and every secret.

But there was another me, also. The me who

seemed to have started kicking and screaming the minute we crossed the bridge into Maine. That me hated those turtles and their ignorant hard hats, which were just like my suitcase brain, crammed full of questions they'd never get answered because just when they ought to be looking, *zoom*, in went their heads.

Think of the things I ought to be dealing with. Facts even a turtle-head couldn't ignore. Facts such as my father had been in this house. He'd been in this house and in this town, and there were probably people who'd known him, but had I asked anyone one question? No.

Facts such as my mother had said, Don't go making connections, like she was hiding from people. Well, she *was* hiding from people, and those people included Fake Man. Was he also hiding from her? Yes, I knew the minute I wondered. I'd seen his face in the window, seen how it looked surprised.

So this mystery was mine, not Roger's. To Roger it was only a game, but to me it was something else. Something bigger—much bigger—and I didn't even know what. Hadn't even been wondering in any real kind of way. Hadn't even told Roger about my mother's knowing Fake Man. Hadn't—oh, anything.

I stared up at those turtles again.

"You are very beautiful," I told them. Because they were. Someone had dotted in all of the details of their shells in these great quiet colors. "But you're just pictures, and you're going nowhere."

And some little part of me poked out of its shell.

I watched the *Emily Ann* swing around and bump against the pier. Okay, I was here. I was watching. I might even be following, miracles did happen.

I watched teenage deckhands toss ropes over the side to a girl hardly older than I was who leaned out over the water to catch them and loop them around the pilings. I couldn't believe how fast she moved, how coolly she did what had to be done without even looking down. I'd be a plunk in the water. I'd—

Suddenly, people were clanking along the gangplank. There was Fake Man! I turned sideways, pretending not to watch when really I was. The man limped, wore a backpack, carried a cardboard carton.

When he got to the road, he stopped and looked around, just like Roger had said he would, studying people to make sure no one was watching. My heart started thumping. I turned back to the boat. Should I do it?

No, I decided, I shouldn't. If he *was* doing something illegal, following him would be stupid, even dangerous. He would be carrying his booty, whatever the booty was.

On the other hand, if my mother had once been

involved with a criminal, I ought to know what kind
of criminal he was. Right?

A man in a brown cap and uniform—the captain,
I guessed—came out of the cabin, onto the deck. His
face was all chapped and wind-burned. I stared at him
like this mattered. Like this was the thing I'd come to
consider. Did the boat go out in the winter? Of course
it did. This one or some other. Roger said people
lived out on that island, somebody had to go out
there. Not this boat, probably. This one was made for
tourists. That mail boat maybe. I tried to imagine the
sea in winter, what the rocking boat would feel like.
The thought made my stomach roll. Roger would
probably do it. He'd go out on a boat in winter. Roger
would go out in a raging storm!

The thought of Roger made me remember why I
was there. I spun around. Fake Man was gone! Without even thinking, I took off running. Which way had
the man gone? I slapped at my leg as I ran. *Idiot!* Some
spy you are.

I rounded the corner and there was Fake Man! I
stopped running and pressed myself into some
bushes, my heart *thump, thump, thump*ing. I listened
to it in surprise—the heartbeat of someone who'd
acted without thinking.

Uh-oh, Fake Man had paused next to the car lot.
What if he got in a car and drove away? *Don't,* I silently
begged, because suddenly, more than anything, I

wanted to follow him, wanted to hear the *thump*, *thump*, *thump* of the mission pounding away in my ears.

He headed on, on foot. Up the hill, past the inn, past the post office, past the churches on the left. I slid out of the bushes and followed. We passed the houses on the edge of the town. We passed Roger's street. What if he turned around? I was wondering, when he did! I threw myself onto a lawn and looked down the hill toward the harbor. Hum, dum, de-dum. I lay back and counted the boats on the water.

When I dared to look up again, the man had disappeared. I hurried onto my feet. This spying business was work.

At the top of the hill, I stopped and looked around. A road led off to the right, into the woods. There the man went, now turning a corner left, no longer limping. Gee, you walk pretty fast for an old person carrying a package, I said to myself. Following him here would be harder. There were no other people, and the road was gravel, which crunched when you walked. I would have to fall back, to follow without actually *seeing* the person I followed. I went on, keeping to the side of the road, but over and over again the branches of trees and bushes kept forcing me into the gravel. *Crunch, crunch.* It was impossible to be quiet.

I walked for a long time. After a while, I began to feel pretty dumb. The only crunching sounds came from my own feet. Fake Man might have turned off anywhere. How could I know?

At that very minute, I heard a noise. I stopped walking and peeked in through the trees to my right. There was an old log building—like a cabin, I guess, only bigger—and there, at its door, stood Fake Man, setting the carton down, taking off his backpack. I started walking again, my heart pounding louder than ever. Stay calm, don't hurry, pretend you do not even see him. Because by now he would have heard my footsteps, would be looking out through the trees.

But when I was out of sight of the cabin, I stopped long enough to raise my fists in the air and hiss out a happy *"Yes!"* Then I bolted.

16

I crashed in through the doorway. Six-thirty on the dot.

Madeleine raised an eyebrow. "Mighty close," she said.

I sank into a chair and wiped my face on my T-shirt. I'd gotten lost trying to find my way out of the woods without passing the cabin again.

"Mighty close," I agreed. It seemed to sum up my life right now: I'd almost been caught, almost been lost, almost been late, and now I was almost starving. Madeleine piled up my plate with spaghetti—meatball-and-mushroom sauce, my favorite!

But then I couldn't eat it. Spaghetti. Ugh. I thought that I might be sick. It was as if the surprise of what I'd been doing for the last hour had chased me all through the woods and finally made it in through the doorway.

"You're not hungry?" Madeleine frowned down at me.

"Well, I thought I was."

She narrowed her eyes and studied me. "You been running. Go take a bath, and soak your sorry self. I'll keep this warm."

The minute she said it, I knew it was just what I wanted to do. I pushed back my chair and stood up. "Thanks."

Madeleine smiled back. "Believe me, the pleasure will be all mine."

Upstairs, I filled the bathtub and sank down into it. Already, I was sore from running. I lay back, liking the swoosh of the water around my ears. I stared up at the walls, which were painted a bright peach. Peach-colored whales swam through the shower curtains. A wave of happiness came over me, as if all the bubbles of water were really bubbles of joy and now they were pop-pop-popping around me. I'd been in Maine for only two days, and look at the things that had happened: I'd made a real friend, spied on a stranger, been lost in the woods and then found my way out again. Earned some sore muscles, and not from gym class, either. From something *real*. When was the last time that happened? Maybe never!

Madeleine had the spaghetti ready when I returned. "So," she said. "That must have been quite an adventure."

This was really a question, I knew. I stuffed spaghetti into my mouth, wondering how I should answer.

"Did you—" But before she could finish the sentence, a tinkling sound drifted down from upstairs.

"What in the heck is that?" I stopped eating to listen. The sound came again. *Tinkle, tinkle.* It was like some kind of a bell.

Madeleine actually blushed. "Your mother," she said. She wiped her hands on a towel. "I didn't want her to have to holler. It hurts her head."

My mouth fell open. My mother was *ringing* for servants now?

"*My* idea," Madeleine hurried to say. "I'm the one who bought her the bell." But she looked embarrassed anyway. She hurried out of the room.

I stared at the spot where she'd been standing. That had *not* been the real Madeleine. The real Madeleine was missing! But just as I thought this, the real Madeleine's head popped back in through the door.

"Where I come from, hollering is too crude. We almost never use it." The bell tinkled again. "*Coming!*" she hollered. She flashed me a smile and left.

I sat there and ate my spaghetti. I thought about a mother who would use a bell. I thought about two fancy minds who'd maybe loved each other to pieces. So my father had been like my mother? Was that what Madeleine had meant when she'd said that?

I closed my eyes and pictured them. There they were: my mother and father. They were sitting in an elegant living room, drinking sherry and smiling and speaking some foreign language. Ringing for servants. No baby was in that room. No baby was in their minds. Those two fancy minds.

Where was the baby? I wondered.

But then I stopped wondering. Nothing would spoil this day. This day would sit in my mind and be perfect: the day I'd popped my shell.

That night, I decided to make a map to the mystery man's cabin. I drew it on a roll of shelf paper I found in my dresser drawer. It unrolled and unrolled, so the map could go on and on and on as the path wound through the woods. I put everything on it—the post office, the inn, the churches. Even boats out on the water. The more I drew, the more I saw how what I was really drawing was happiness. I was drawing my perfect day. It's amazing to me when that happens, when your drawing lays it right out there, what you are feeling. And it's interesting *how*. I mean, it wasn't like I was drawing smiley faces or something. The happiness was in the shapes and the lines of the buildings, in things you can't really explain. You just looked at the picture and *felt* it.

Weirdest of all is when what you are drawing shows you what you are feeling when you don't even know you feel it. Like this one time, I was drawing this valuable vase that my mother owns? My whole life, I'd believed it when my mother told me that vase was beautiful. Rare, precious, beautiful. I might have started out drawing it like that, but before I knew it, I was turning its handles into big fat old wrinkled arms and giving it this weird sort of face that looked kind of evil. And you know what? For the first time, I saw how that vase was ugly. Yep. Precious or not, the vase was ugly. My drawing had told me the truth.

Which is why I liked to keep my drawings private. What they will tell you, they will also tell other people. Not that other people will care. When I was little, I showed my mother my drawings. She looked at them. Didn't comment. They disappeared. Well, forget that. I don't draw to make things disappear. I draw to keep them alive. What made this map unusual was that I was drawing for another person. I was making it for Roger. I knew he would like it, too. I'd drawn his cool house and put his face in an upstairs window. Just the top of his face, because he was spying.

Roger! I'd forgotten to call him.

I opened my door a crack and peeked into the hallway. My mother's door was closed. So was Madeleine's. Being as quiet as I could on the squeaking and squonking stairs, I tiptoed down to the kitchen and made my phone call.

"Sweeney machiney," Roger's voice said. "Say something important after the beep."

"Hi, Roger, this is William. Talk to you later." I smiled and hung up. I guessed Roger would think that was important, all right.

"Gee," said a voice on the sunporch. "Sounds like we got us some company. I wonder what William will want for breakfast."

I swallowed hard and stared toward the darkened porch, smiling this bright phony smile in case I could be seen. "Gee," I answered. "I think he prefers pancakes."

"Gotcha," the voice answered.

Great. Just what every spy wants to hear.

But I went on being happy, anyway. I was happy that whole night. Which, for me, was probably a record.

Doctor Winthrop

It is widely proclaimed that I am a brilliant person. Renowned in the field of linguistics, emphasis on semantics. Semantics, in which context reigns supreme. Ironic, isn't it? That my brain can accept that language is fluid — that a word will mean one thing if used in one time and place, and something else if used in another — and yet refuse to acknowledge change.

I reject fluidity.

I want life to be as it was.

I want my husband back.

I want, as my son, that smiling baby who needs me instead of the one who hides in his room drawing pictures, thinking that I don't know.

I was wrong to come back to Maine. This house is too full of ghosts, and my son stirs them up. He brings them in from the town on the soles of his feet. His very face in the chair across from me sets them dancing and makes me weak.

Why did I come here? I wanted to believe that I could move forward into a future that's free of the past. But ghosts are tyrants.

There's a stillness now in the house.

There's an unearthly feeling of stillness.

I believe it's my own ghost who haunts me.

It is, I can see it clearly. It's the ghost of a person who once was happy.

17

I couldn't *wait* to get to Roger's house the next morning. Whatever the next part of the plan was, I was pretty sure I could do it. It was another bright blue I-can-do-anything morning in Maine.

But first, I had to check out the ten-thirty boat and make sure Fake Man was on it. Spying on him today would be different from doing it yesterday now that Fake Man might have seen me, but I wasn't afraid. Careful, but not afraid. I hid behind a Dumpster.

It was busy on the boat landing. The *Sarah Blue* was being unloaded while the *Emily Ann* was being loaded. I watched piles of cartons and backpacks and suitcases coming off and going on. I wondered if they ever made a mistake and loaded the unloaded pile back onto the other boat. Maybe there was really only one big load of stuff that went around and around, back and forth to the island, year after year, never really landing. I smiled. Whoops, there was Fake Man! I ducked back and peeked out.

Fake Man was doing what I was doing, which was

keeping a low profile. He was standing behind a pickup truck, watching the *Sarah Blue*. A big wooden crate was being unloaded. Man, look at the size of that thing. It was obviously heavy, taking three men to maneuver it. Over the gangplank, out through the crowd, straight to the pickup truck where Fake Man was hiding. He was watching it, I was watching it, *yow*, our eyes almost met!

I ducked down and stayed down. From behind the Dumpster, I listened while the captain give his welcome-aboard talk. I heard the crowd tramping over the gangplank. But how could I see if Fake Man was part of that crowd if I wasn't looking? Slowly, I made myself look. Fake Man's head was not in the sea of bobbing heads. But here he came, all by himself, limping toward the gangplank, carrying his carton. He was the last person to get on. The boat horn sounded. The ropes were cast off. The boat pulled away from the pier. He was on, he was gone. Mission accomplished.

Roger opened the door smiling. "William, I presume? William the Conqueror?"

I smiled back and clicked my heels (well, okay, I bonked them since I was wearing sneakers) and took a bow. "At your service."

Inside, we spread the map on the dining room

table and anchored its corners with books. I felt shy, watching Roger's eyes wander around it, but he appreciated it, just like I'd known he would.

"Holy cow!" He turned to look at me, his face all bright with respect. "Homer, this thing is awesome!"

I did my best to look modest. "Thanks." But I had to admit it was true. The map had turned into a work of art. My best one ever.

"This is so cool! Hey, look at my house! And me! And here's the—" His finger was walking the map. Suddenly, it stopped. Roger looked up at me. "This is it? This is where Fake Man lives?" His finger tapped at the cabin circled in red.

I nodded. "Yes. Why? You know the place?"

Roger shrugged and tried to look cool, but I could tell he was sort of shaken. "Well, sure. It's just an empty old place. Little kids call it the Spookety Cabin."

"Spookety? As in haunted?"

"Well, I guess. It's just a place nobody goes."

"But somebody *does* go there," I said.

Roger looked at me. "Yeah. Someone who needs a place to hide. Because that's what you do if you're a criminal. And where's a better place to hide than a place where nobody goes?"

We stared at each other awhile. The back of my neck started tingling.

"So how come nobody goes there?" I asked.

"I don't know. It's just, like, bad vibes. The last person who lived there took off years ago and never came back. Didn't even try to sell the place. So now it's just falling down. And that's how it's always been. Abandoned. Creepy. It's one of the oldest places on the peninsula, but nobody has ever lived in it. Or at least not for long. Which makes you wonder, you know? Plus it, well, it just sort of *feels* funny when you're there."

"You've been there?"

"Everybody's *been* there. You just don't hang around. But I'll do it," he added. "I'll do it because we need to."

Did we? Yes, I supposed we did. If we were going to crack the Fake Man mystery, we were going to have to check out the place where he lived.

"In fact, we're going up there now," Roger said.

"We are?"

"We are. Ready?"

"Aye, aye," I answered, giving a salute. "I mean, roger, Roger!"

Roger smiled and saluted back. "Cool. I mean, homer, Homer!"

18

"We're not breaking and entering, right?" I asked on the way to the cabin. There were pains in my stomach and chest, weird jabbing pains, the kind that might go with a heart attack.

"Of course not," Roger answered. "I mean, not unless we have to."

The pain shot into my neck.

"I mean, if things look really suspicious—like maybe *he* broke and entered—well, then maybe we'll have to."

I'm not doing it, I decided. I am *not* breaking and entering.

Roger watched my face as we walked, reading the cowardly things it was saying. "Probably we won't have to," he added.

It was *not* being cowardly to not want to break the law, I told myself. I might be a coward in lots of things, but this wasn't one of them. I was here, wasn't I? I was walking along beside Roger, heading for a place called the Spookety Cabin.

"You know," Roger said, after we'd walked for a long time without talking, "that map you made was awesome."

"Really?" The pains settled down into a mild sort of rumble.

"Really. Do you think you could make me some others? Like, maybe one with the shortcuts from my house to yours. Not that we need it, of course." He blushed, as if he'd said something childish.

I blushed, too. "Sure."

Suddenly, Roger pointed. There it was—the cabin.

Both of us looked behind us. Nobody else was in sight. No sound of feet or cars on the gravel. Slowly, we made our way through the trees and bushes. Branches scratched at my arms and T-shirt. I couldn't feel those branches. I couldn't feel my own feet when they touched the ground. *Why* was I doing this? I wondered but couldn't remember.

Roger stopped. I stopped behind him.

We both stared up at the cabin. Yep, spookety was the word. It was big for a cabin—long, and two stories high. It all sort of tipped to one side as if the vines climbing up it were pulling it down. Tree branches pressed against it. The bottom front windows were boarded over. In my humble opinion, no one would live here unless he had something to hide. A padlock the size of Texas hung from the door. Good luck getting into *this* place. Not that I wanted to.

Roger whistled softly.

I nodded. It would be dark inside, I was thinking. It would be totally black in that place. For a second, the sky seemed to be less blue.

Roger looked at me. "We'll need a flashlight."

Maybe *he'd* need a flashlight. *I* wasn't going inside.

"Which means we'll have to come back."

"Yes." Which meant we could leave right now.

Roger took off, but not in the direction I had in mind. He disappeared around the side of the cabin.

I stared where he had gone. He didn't come back. I didn't want to go around the cabin, but I also didn't want to stand there all alone.

"Homer, come here!"

I went.

Roger was standing in what had once been a backyard but was now a jungle of weeds and bushes and a few stray flowers. "Check it out. The windows back here aren't boarded up. They—"

Suddenly, we heard a sound—the sound of a car coming through the woods. *A car?* It couldn't be, but it was. Closer and closer it came. At the same moment, Roger and I noticed the rutted path that cut through the woods and ended practically where we stood. A driveway!

We dove into the bushes just as a pickup truck

roared into the yard. It kept on coming, crashing through bushes and brush as it came. It drove right up to the cabin and stopped.

"Don't move," Roger whispered.

As if I would move. As if I *could*. I'd become one with the earth, smelling dirt.

The truck doors slammed. There was clanging and scraping and grunting. A man's voice said, "Wait, watch it!" Then the sounds moved away.

"Did you see them?" Roger asked.

Not likely. I rolled over and sat up.

"Keep down," he said. "Here they come!"

I froze again, but this time I was in a position to peek through a hole in the bushes. I saw feet. I saw cardboard cartons. I saw hands lift those cartons up.

"Stay here," a voice said. "I'll go get the rest of it."

One set of feet walked off. The other stayed there. They stayed and they stayed.

A mosquito landed on my arm. I sat as still as a person could sit and still be breathing. Maybe I wasn't breathing!

And then . . . Roger farted.

We stared at each other. Saw the feet turn around.

"Run!" Roger hissed.

We ran, all right. Back through the bushes, on, on down the road, sending the gravel flying behind us. We ran until my feet were numb. I thought I would burst if I didn't stop running, but my feet kept on going and going as if they were too numb to follow orders to stop.

At the first sight of a lawn, Roger crashed onto the grass. I followed him. We lay there panting, unable to speak. I didn't even want to speak. I wanted nothing, except to breathe, and suddenly I couldn't do that. My chest felt hard, like a barrel of rocks. Pain stabbed through it. A heart attack for certain!

I closed my eyes. I was dying—*dying*, that's how it honestly felt, the pain was so sharp and so throbbing, so like a heart that was trying to beat.

But I didn't die. Slowly, my breath came back to me. The feeling returned to my feet, my barrel of a chest got soft again. I stared up at the sky over my head. Still blue, it was, with fluffy white clouds sailing through it. Somewhere a bird chirped. Suddenly, I felt happy, the way I'd felt in the bathtub and when I was drawing my map. *Happy*, when what we'd just done had been crazy, maybe dangerous. When men in a truck might be coming to find us.

Roger started laughing. He laughed and he laughed. "They should put that in the spying hand-book," he squeaked out. "No cold chili dogs for breakfast."

I started laughing, too. Because that's how life is with Roger. You're spying, you're dying, you're laughing.

19

"We'd better get out of sight," Roger said when he'd finally stopped laughing. "You know, in case they saw as well as heard us." One final round of snickers, and then we crossed the street to the park, where we could sit behind bushes.

The park wasn't much by Boston standards. A small black-topped area with a basketball hoop. A jungle gym. Two benches. Roger and I plopped down on one of them.

"Oh, man," Roger said with a sigh. "That was really not funny. Something's up at that cabin, all right."

"What were they doing?" I asked. "I couldn't really see. Could you?"

"I couldn't see faces, but I saw what they were doing. They were carrying out cartons. Cartons exactly like Fake Man carries. And they took in a crate. One of those big wooden ones you build to fit what you need to ship. There was this black X painted on the bottom. Must have been heavy. They were groaning like crazy."

I stared at him. I'd seen a crate with an X painted on the bottom, but it hadn't been at the cabin. "Roger, this morning when I went to see Fake Man get on the boat, they were taking a crate like that off of the *Sarah Blue*. Some men loaded it onto a pickup truck. And Fake Man was watching, I'm sure of it."

Roger stared back at me. "No way! A delivery from Owl Island goes straight to the cabin—a delivery with an X on it instead of a name—and our man who wears a disguise is watching over it? Homer, if Fake Man is a smuggler, then what we just saw—" Suddenly, his eyes got big. "Duck!"

I ducked. A truck roared down the hill from the direction we'd just come. It rounded the corner and went by.

Roger sat up slowly. His face had gone white. "That was them," he whispered.

"But they didn't see us. Right?"

He looked right at me. "No. But I saw them."

"And...?"

"And I knew one of them! It was Freddy, the captain's son!"

"The captain? You mean, as in the *Emily Ann*?"

"The one. Geez." His brow wrinkled into a frown. He stared down at the ground.

"What does that mean?" I asked. The expression

on his face was changing from thoughtful to sad to angry, then back again to thoughtful and on again to sad. "Roger?"

"You aren't going to believe this," he said finally. The expression had settled in somewhere between thoughtful and sad. "I think the captain is in on whatever's going on."

He was right, I didn't believe it. It was a pretty big leap from seeing the captain's son to believing *that*.

"I know, I know! It sounds crazy. But listen, there are things I haven't told you. For example. I've never once seen Fake Man hand over a boarding pass when he gets on that boat. Have you? Did he have one this morning?"

I thought about it. No. He'd walked straight onto the boat. I shook my head.

"Right. And who else gets to carry a package that big on with him? Nobody, that's who. They load the baggage on separately."

That was true, too. I'd watched them do it this morning. "But—but—"

"But why didn't I tell you sooner?" He shrugged. His expression tipped closer to sad. "Because this is *the captain* we're talking about. A man who's been, like, the captain forever. You know what I mean?"

I knew. I understood perfectly. Roger had come across some facts he did not want to deal with, so he'd thrown them into his brain and slammed down the lid and now that lid was coming up. Roger had a suitcase in his brain, too! This thought made me so happy somewhere deep down inside that I almost smiled, but I squashed the happiness. Or I saved it for later. Right now, I felt sorry for Roger.

"There might be some explanation," I said. "Sometimes things aren't what they seem." But sometimes, of course, they were. And sometimes you didn't have a clue whether they were or they weren't, and you had to work to find out. "We'll have to just go with the facts here. Try not to be influenced by what we think we already know. That's what good spies would do."

Roger nodded. "Yes. Go with the facts. The facts look bad, don't they?"

I thought about it for a while. "Yes," I said. "They do."

20

"Homer?" Madeleine! I threw my drawing pad into the drawer of my desk and slammed it shut. I'd been sitting there since dinnertime trying to draw a picture of the feet I'd seen through the bushes, but I couldn't get them right. The feet had looked *scary*, and how did a foot do that?

"Yeah? I mean, yes?"

She opened the door and stuck her head in. "There's a phone call for you." She was saying it quietly, so my mother wouldn't hear her. "Your new acquaintance, I reckon."

I hurried down the stairs, *squonch*, *creak*.

"Homer?" Roger sounded breathless. "You've got to get over here early in the morning. I've got stuff to tell you. Major stuff."

"Stuff like what?"

"Can't tell you on the phone. Just get over here. My mother's going into Stonehaven before she goes to work, so any time after eight. The earlier the better. Okay?"

"Sure. Okay. See you." The phone went dead.

"Was that your new friend?" Madeleine whispered as I passed her room. She was in there polishing my mother's shoes. As if my mother needed shoes. As if her feet would walk her anywhere except to bed until we got back to Boston.

I nodded and stepped inside so my mother wouldn't hear me. "Yes. Roger. He wants me to come over again tomorrow. Is it okay—all right—if I go?" I smiled, and I swear I did not feel one bit of guilt for the parts I wasn't telling. I had feet that *did* want to walk, and Madeleine, well, she understood that.

"Sure, sugar, thanks for asking." And she went back to shining the shoes, her face as bright and cheerful as if she were polishing up her diamonds.

"You ought to go see the lighthouse," I told her. "It's beautiful there. It's the best place in Herring Cove."

She looked up at me, her hand, holding the brush, still moving back and forth over a shoe. "You know, maybe I will." She smiled. "One of these mornings, I'll get up bright and early and go see me the lighthouse."

Roger opened the door the second I crossed his porch, his face its firecracker self. I felt a bubble of worry, that he might have solved the mystery of Fake Man without me.

"What's so important?" I said.

He waved me in and slammed the door behind me. "Homer, last night I told my mother your name, and you should have seen her face."

"Why? How did it look?"

"Surprised. Like she had heard it before. Then she starts asking me all these questions. Like where are you staying, and who's up here with you. I told her Madeleine, you, and your mother—there's only the three of you, right?—and how you're staying down in the village. 'His *mother*?' she says. 'You mean *Catherine* is here?' And her eyebrows shoot up to the sky. Catherine's your mother, right?"

"Well, nobody calls her that. She's always Doctor Winthrop." Why? I wondered for the first time. Didn't my mother have any friends? "But it is her name."

"That's what I thought!" Roger was so excited his hair was practically standing on end. "So I say to her, 'Hey, you *know* Homer's mother?' and she gets this funny look on her face and says, 'Well, Roger, I don't know the answer to that.' Now what does *that* mean? Either you know someone or you don't."

Not necessarily. We were talking about my mother here.

"And get this. While I'm getting ready for bed, brushing my teeth, I ask, sort of casual-like, 'So, what's the story with the Spookety Cabin? How come nobody ever lives in it very long?' And my mother, whoa, she turns the color of toothpaste, and *whomp*, down comes this hand on my shoulder—I don't mean a friendly hand, either, I mean the other kind—and she says, 'Roger, have you taken Homer out to that cabin?' I say no, because I didn't *take* you out there, right? You went on your own two feet. She thinks for a minute and then says, 'Roger, you keep Homer away from that place. Take him fishing or something.' And it's like she means *you*, personally. Not just any kid. When I ask why, all she'll say is, 'Because I said so. Now get the lead out and go to bed.' Which I did, since she doesn't talk when she gets like that. Plus, my shoulder was starting to feel like lobster bait. Homer, maybe you were never here before, but your mother sure was. She was maybe even connected somehow with the cabin."

"Roger, I *have* been here before. We came here when I was a baby. And do you know what my mother did when she heard about *you*?"

He raised his eyebrows and shook his head.

"She flipped out. She said, 'Homer, don't go making connections. Don't announce that we're here.' Said she didn't want *'visitors'* from her past."

"Wow! So then they *did* know each other! Why don't they want to see each other, then?"

"Don't know," I managed to say. I was thinking about how the look on my mother's face hadn't really been about Roger. It had been about *any* friends. My guess was she was hiding from everyone in this town and that everyone in town would know her name for some reason. What awful thing could make a grown-up woman hide from a whole town? Something impossible to imagine.

Trouble was . . . I was starting to imagine it.

Something big. Something dark. Something ugly.

21

"**M**an, this is wild." Roger's eyes were like saucers. "Homer, if you were here before, and our mothers knew each other, then we might have been friends as babies. And doesn't that make this all freaky, like destiny? I mean, here I was following Fake Man, and then he leads you out to the cabin, and now maybe that cabin's connected to *you*, and maybe we were connected as babies!"

Fake Man. Uh-oh. "Roger, there's something I haven't told you."

"There is? What?"

"Well, there probably *is* a connection between me and the cabin, because I think my mother knows Fake Man."

Roger blinked. "*Knows* him? Knows him as in—*how*? You mean like—they're *friends* or something?"

"Well, yeah, or enemies."

Roger just stared at me.

I told him everything—how we were riding along in the car, how Fake Man's face had appeared in the fog—all of it, shooting it out in one big long breath, hoping he'd just jump right in on the mystery and not worry about the whys or the whens of the telling.

No such luck. Roger's face, well, let's just say that it didn't look friendly.

"I know, I know," I admitted. "I should have told you sooner."

"Gee, now why would you think that? Just because we've been talking about the man since the second you got here? Or no, since the second you told me that *you'd never been here before.* Yeah, since then."

I felt myself turning red. "Roger, I meant I didn't *remember* I'd been here before. Which I didn't. And anyhow, I only found out in the car on the way up here how I'd been here when I was a baby and how we own the house and all that. When I met you, it still wasn't feeling real. It still doesn't."

"How you *own the house and all that?*"

I sighed. "I guess I forgot to tell you that also. But, Roger, it was like your not telling me about the captain. You know? Some information just sounds so crazy that you don't know what to do with it. Sort of like, where to put it inside of your brain. So you don't put it anywhere. Or you throw it into your suitcase and let it just sit there."

"Your *suitcase?*" But now he did what I'd hoped he would do. He stopped looking mad and fell into the mystery. He squinted up at the ceiling. "Homer, think about all of this. Your mom owns a house and she never comes up here. Never tells you about it. Then, when she does come, she tells you not to go talking to people—people like *me*, whose mom has, in fact, been asking questions. Plus she knows a man who wears a *disguise*? And she looks *scared* when she sees him? Those are pretty bizarre facts!"

I nodded. No need to tell me that the facts were bizarre. But hearing them lined up like that, hearing them said by another person, well, let's just say the lid on my suitcase was up, it was just plain up. Anything might happen, and I would be ready to hear it. Okay, maybe not ready. But I wouldn't slam down the lid again. That's the only way I can describe it, the way things changed for good.

Roger was still staring over my head. You could practically hear gears churning.

"And now, on top of everything else, I'm supposed to keep you away from the cabin. A cabin where something suspicious has been going on. The cabin that's home to Fake Man, the man who connects us all."

The man who connects us all. I hated those words. A *fake* man connected me to my mother.

"Come on," I said to Roger.

"Why? Where are we going?" But he knew.

22

On the way to the cabin, Roger stopped walking. "Homer, we forgot!"

"Forgot what?" I felt this twinge, this sort of goosebumpy feeling, like I'd probably forgotten a lot, but I kept on moving. Nothing could stop me now, my own usual cowardly self included.

Roger hurried to catch up. "To make sure Fake Man got on the boat." Whoops, minor detail. The twinge turned into a bomb that sort of blew off the top of my head. But it was funny, all the goosebumpy feelings blew away with it.

"He's on it," I said to Roger. Not that I really knew. I was just way past being careful. Being careful was somewhere up in the air, glued to the top of my head.

"How do you know that? You don't! It's only just ten-thirty."

"If he's at the cabin, we'll deal with it."

"And what if the truck comes back? What if—"

"We'll deal with it," I repeated.

Roger fell silent.

"Roger's Law rules," I said. "Aren't you Roger?" Which probably sounded rude. Which *was* rude. I wasn't thinking about Roger Sweeney. I was thinking about Homer Winthrop and how he would do anything, any old thing at all. If someone said, "Homer, you have to blow up that cabin to get at the truth," then I'd blow it up. Because that place was packed full of secrets, and at least some of those secrets were *mine*.

Fake Man wasn't there. The padlock on the door of the cabin was snapped tight. Roger and I stared at the cabin awhile. I remembered what Roger had been saying when the truck had roared onto the scene. The windows in back weren't boarded up.

"I'm going in," I decided. No comment from Roger, but he followed me around to the back of the cabin.

I stared at the windows. Not only were they not boarded up, there didn't seem to be any locks on them.

"We need something to stand on," I said. The minute I said it, I saw what the something would be. A broken-down picnic table sat by the edge of the woods. I headed over to check it out.

It was wobbly, but it would work. I started pulling it, bouncing and creaking, across the bumpy ground.

"Come help me," I called to Roger. He hadn't

moved a muscle to help, and he didn't move now. I turned and looked at him, and I swear, it was Homer the Chicken standing there. Any minute now, he'd start clucking.

"Never mind," I called, pretending I didn't notice. "It isn't that heavy." Which was a lie, but I pulled the table all the way by myself, just like it *wasn't* heavy. I knew about being a chicken. You didn't need witnesses.

When the table was where I wanted it, I climbed up and examined the window. Just as I'd thought, no lock. But the window was stuck shut. It wasn't going to budge.

Behind me, I heard Roger take a deep breath. "I'll help," he said. The table wobbled, and he was there. Together we pushed. No use.

We moved to the next window. This one wiggled a little in its frame, but it wasn't going up, either.

Roger stared at me. "You're serious, right? You're going in? Breaking and entering?"

"I'm going in. Breaking and entering." I didn't like the sound of the words, but I thought I might as well say them, they were the truth.

We looked at each other awhile. I could see the Chicken in him getting weaker. Solve-Every-Mystery-Roger was in there stomping on its puny guts.

"Okay," Real Roger said finally. "What we need is a stick. Something we can put up against the frame and push on together. That way, both of us will be using our strength in the same place." He hopped down from the table. He looked around and came back with a small board.

"This'll work." One end of the board propped against the window frame, one end propped against us. "Okay," he said. *"Push!"*

We pushed. There was the sound of smashing glass. Roger and I fell against each other.

"Whoa!" Roger straightened up and shook the sprinkles of glass off his hands and arms.

"Whoops." I did the same.

We examined the window. Smashed, totally smashed. The one large piece of glass that still hung in the frame crashed to the table the second that Roger touched it, missing our feet by about an inch.

We looked at each other.

"That wasn't the kind of breaking I had in mind," I said.

But breaking had happened. So. Now it was time for entering.

Trash in the Suitcase, Uh-oh

If Homer's brain was:

(and that's his own descriptio

Then mine was this:

And Homer actually admired that! I guess you can get tired of being neat.

So this one day Homer starts thinking like me. Then he starts acting like me. Which really freaks me out, because it's different when you're the one being reckless, since you know how far you will go. Guess what? It turns _me_ into a chicken!

So picture this.

I'm part Homer.

He's part me

Which is kind of neat, don't you think?
It makes us like blood brothers.
But it also made us a little crazy.

We broke a few laws.

We broke
a few promises.

We broke a window.

Oops.

We didn't mean to
do any of those
things. And we will
never do them
again....

Unless we need to.

13

Entering, of course, was easy. Roger took a stick and ran it along the edge of the window frame to rub off the rough edges of glass, and we simply climbed in.

"Man, look at this place," Roger whispered when we were inside. "It's a pit!"

My eyes were adjusting to the darkness. It *was* a pit. Part of a ceiling had caved in. There were old broken chairs turned upside down and a table buried under a pile of plaster dust. "Phew." I held my nose.

"Mold," Roger said. "And maybe a dead animal." He wandered on, into the next room. The Chicken was definitely history.

"Hey, Homer, come look at this!"

I followed him. In the next room, there were sawhorses and a pile of lumber. A bucket of nails.

"Somebody's working in here. Or at least they're planning to. And, hey, come check this out." He was off again, into what remained of an old kitchen. It was in the front of the house, where the windows were boarded up. I stood in the doorway, waiting for my eyes to adjust again.

"Totally trashed," he said.

Trashed was the word, all right. The sink had been pulled out from the wall and disconnected from its plumbing. In the center of the room, there was a pile of big green garbage bags, all filled and stinking. No way was I going in there. I backed out of the doorway.

"He can't be living in this place," I said to Roger, when he appeared again. "*No one* could live here. Not even Fake Man."

"Not even *me*," he agreed. "Hey, there's an upstairs. Maybe he's living up there. Let's find the staircase."

We found it, but I didn't like it. It went up, rounded a corner, and disappeared into total darkness.

"I hate this," I admitted when we'd started climbing, Roger in front, me holding onto his shirt.

"Me, too! I'm breaking cobwebs up here."

"Which means Fake Man doesn't use these steps. So let's turn around." But Roger didn't stop. He was back to being Roger, all right. I guess I was back to being Homer, because I was thinking, What if those smugglers come back while we're upstairs? Ahead of me, there was a thumping and bumping and a door flew open.

The upstairs was even worse than the downstairs,

if that was possible. There was garbage all over the place. Broken furniture, old tin cans, a pair of gross-looking shoes. Smelly mattresses that had been dragged around on the floor. A bird had made a nest in the middle of one of them.

"Hey, home!" Roger said brightly.

"I'm getting out of here," I decided. In two seconds flat, I was back down the steps. What was this mess teaching us? Nothing. Only that Fake Man couldn't possibly be living in a place this awful, so he *had* to be using it for some other shady purpose. We were right about that. And what could my mother have to do with a man like that? Nothing. My mother might have a secret, but her secret wasn't *this*. This part was all some giant, dumb misunderstanding. "I'm leaving!" I called up the stairs.

But I didn't leave. I stood in the middle of what must have once been a living room and waited for Roger. Right in front of me was a closed door. I stared at it. A room we hadn't gone into? Yes. And I knew while I stared that this was the room that would matter.

Slowly, I walked over to the door. I pushed it open.

This room was clean. There was a mattress on the floor with sheets on it. A little table with a neat row of cups. A bottle of water. The crate, but now it was open and empty.

I took a step into the room. A small dresser with a mirror attached. A hook with a pair of pants. Three cardboard cartons with their tops neatly folded in. Cartons like Fake Man carried! Now was our chance to find out what was inside them. I took a few more steps inside.

I stopped again. Across the room stood a statue. Or the beginnings of a statue. It was only a piece of stone with a face and a hand and a toe sticking out, but I knew at once that it was much more than that. It was real and alive and looking right at me. At *me*, Homer Aldrich Winthrop. *Help!* it called. *Come closer, I need you!*

So I went closer. I stared into those eyes. Sad, begging eyes that had something important to say to me. And that something was huge, bigger than anything I'd ever known. It was as if every person who'd ever lived on this earth was stuck somewhere inside the statue. They were stuck and they wanted out, and if I didn't look and listen they wouldn't get out. You could hear them all crying and pounding inside the stone, saying, *Let me out of here!*

So I did look and I did listen. My eyes wandered up and down the statue. It isn't finished, I thought at first, but I knew as soon as I thought it that yes, it was. Whoever had made it wanted to show you what trapped looked like. To show you how life was work. How you had to push your way out of stone, and maybe sometimes you didn't make it. But you had to want to, you just did, or else you'd spend your life being stuck inside stone. You'd spend your life being Homer the Chicken. Or Homer the Suitcase Brain. Or Homer the Turtle. You had to want to *see* things and *do* things and *know* things and *be* things.

And I *do*, I thought. That hand was my hand! That hand wanted to reach out and touch all the things that the eyes saw. It wanted to draw them, I bet anything.

24

"Wow!" Roger said from the doorway. "Fake Man's hideout! You found it!" He came into the room and stopped. He looked at the open crate. He looked at the statue. "Hey, I know that thing. It used to be out on Owl Island. It sat on the little green in front of the church. What's it doing here?"

Talking with me, I wanted to say but didn't.

"That's what was in that crate. Oh my gosh, Homer, that's it! Fake Man is smuggling *art*!"

Art? Off of an *island*?

As usual, Roger saved me the trouble of having to ask. "Owl Island is an artists' colony. It has been, for like, centuries. There must be a million works of art out there, stuck away in all kinds of places."

Artists got to live in colonies? I pictured a group of artists, swarming over a hill like ants, scrambling for the best views. I felt a thrill at the very thought.

"Duh, dumb me." Roger slapped his forehead. "I can't believe that I didn't think of it." He walked around the statue, looking it up and down. Suddenly, he stopped walking. He looked up at me.

"What's the matter?" I asked. I could actually *see* thoughts whirling behind his eyes, but, being me and not Roger, I couldn't read them, and he didn't answer.

"Roger? What is it?"

"Homer—" He sounded out of breath. "Homer—"

"*What?*"

He just pointed at the back of the statue.

I walked around and looked where he was pointing. I saw my name scratched into the stone. *My name?* I couldn't believe my eyeballs.

"What does it mean?" Roger asked in a whisper.

He was asking me? We both stared at the words. There they were: Homer Winthrop.

"I know," Roger said finally. "You were named after your father, weren't you?"

I was.

"I should have known, with a name like Homer." Roger was looking relieved. "So this is *his* signature."

I stared at it. I guessed it had to be. But I'd never seen my father's signature on stone or on paper. Now think about that. Think how you'd feel if you'd never seen your father's signature and hadn't *noticed* you hadn't seen it until you actually did.

"Check it out! It says Owl Island under the signature."

Owl Island? Where Fake Man went on the boat?

"So I'm guessing your father was an artist, right? And he must have lived out on Owl Island. And he carved this statue."

My father had been an artist and lived out on Owl Island? *My father had carved this statue?*

Suddenly, I had to get out of that cabin. I had to get out *fast*—to be out in the air, where my brain could explode with this news in private. I charged through the door, back through the rooms full of garbage, back to the window. *Whomp*, down onto the bench, *plop*, onto the ground, *crash*, through the bushes, this time right through the heart of them, the branches flipping and slapping and tearing at my skin.

My father carved that statue! My father carved that statue! My father carved that statue! Those words were shooting around in my head, like rockets, or firecrackers sending sparks into my gut and even my fingers and even my toes.

I kept on running and running. Never mind the pain that came into my side and into my barrel chest. I didn't care about pain or anything. I just kept seeing that statue and thinking how it had eyes that were burning to see things and a hand that was itching to paint. How whoever was trapped inside that stone was an artist, *like me*!

I stopped running and gasped for breath, seeing the truth pop up right in front of me. There it was, as clear and as true as that statue: I, Homer Winthrop the second, was like Homer Winthrop the first. My father had been an artist, and *I* was an artist. There'd been one other person on earth who saw things and felt things like I did, and no one had ever told me. No one had ever said "Homer, you're just like your father." Because if they had, it would have made all the difference, I know it would have.

I hated my mother. I hated her clean and new, as if I had just been born, as if the hatred I'd already felt had only been baby practice. I hate, hate, hated her. And I was mad at the rest of the world, too. For no particular reason. It just felt good.

25

Madeleine was in the kitchen washing windows when I came storming through the door.

"Howdy," she said. *Howdy*, like I was a normal sight!

I folded my arms and glared at her. "Where's my mother?"

Her arm stopped whirling. She gave me this funny look, a look like, Why Homer, you already know the answer to that. "Up in bed, sick as a dog, same as when you left here. Goodness, let me have a look at them scratches!"

"No!" I folded my arms tighter.

Then Madeleine did the one thing I didn't expect. She went back to washing windows, *squirt, squirt, swipe*.

I stood there watching her work, wishing she'd fall off that stool and break a leg, or at least an ankle.

"I know you're itching to help me," she said cheerfully. "But these windows are mine, all mine. Don't even trouble yourself asking."

Ha, ha, funny. "Well, when is she getting up?"

Madeleine's arm stopped swirling. She squinted down at me for a minute and then stepped off the stool. "Homer, what bug of meanness has took a bite out of you?"

"Stop changing the subject, you old rat!"

I couldn't believe I'd said it, but I had, and I wasn't taking it back!

I couldn't believe the next thing I did, either. I crashed up the stairs to my room, threw myself down on my bed, and started crying. I cried and I cried and I cried. I cried so loudly my mother heard me and actually got out of her bed.

"Go away!" I hollered. Because now I did not want to see her—later I *would*, and then she had better watch out!—but not right now.

Did she go away? No, she didn't. She came into my room like she'd been invited.

"Homer, what on earth is the matter? What's happened to you?" She sat down on the side of my bed and ran her finger over my scratches, making them burn.

Now, I guess I should have sat up right then and asked her my lifetime supply of questions. Asked in a nice way, while *she* was being nice, which might have gotten me some answers. But nice wasn't in me right then. I wanted to lie there and cry and hate her and feel sorry for Homer Winthrop who'd had a father—a father who'd been like *him*!—and then had lost him.

So here's what I did instead:

I said, "Cut it out!" and yanked my arm away.

I said, "*You* happened, you old witch!"

I rolled myself up in a blanket and refused to come out until finally she left me alone. I stayed alone all day. Didn't go down to the phone when Roger called me. Didn't go down when my stomach rumbled. My scratches got ugly and crusty but not really infected. Later, Madeleine set a supper tray inside my door. I didn't touch it.

But I did get up. This will sound kind of weird, but I got up and sat at my desk and made the best map you ever saw. I took a brown paper bag and cut it open and made the edges all jagged and crinkly so it looked sort of old. Then I started to draw, squinting my aching eyes.

I drew all the houses and roads and trees and the lobster boats out on the water. I drew a truck backing a boat to the landing. I drew tourists. I drew an artist sitting up on the hill painting a picture of what must be my own house. Which made me feel kind of funny. Who was this artist? Me? My father? Don't know, just an artist. And had my father actually *been* an artist and not a neurologist?

I drew a dog wading in the water. I drew the cat who begged on the deck at the store. I drew two little skunks I'd seen in the yard last night, poking around in the darkness. These weren't objects most people put on a map, but to me they were objects that ought to be there—not just the bones of a place, but the whole body, with clothing and all. And anyhow, wasn't it useful to know where a neighborhood's skunks lived?

No, probably it wasn't. Thinking this made me stop drawing and stare down at my map. Skunks wandered off. So did tourists. So did artists. For one terrible minute, I wanted to tear that map right up. Nothing on it was useful. Nothing on any map was. A useful map would show you the mysteries inside of houses and the secrets inside of heads. It would show you the people who'd lived in a place before you and the ones who were going to come after—sort of give you a bigger picture, so you could figure out how you fit. It would just go on and do it all—solve every mystery on earth so that people wouldn't have to. You'd be born and you'd open your map and see it: your "You Are Here" arrow. There, marked in red, would be your path. Who'd need a mother? No one.

I wanted a map like that.

I lay down on my bed again. I stayed there a long, long time, until it started to get dark. I heard Madeleine come up the stairs. I heard my mother go into the bathroom.

After a while, I got up and turned on a light and stared at my map. That's when it came to me, what to do. I sat down at my desk. Carefully, one by one, I neatly erased all the roads and paths. I erased and erased, leaving the people and buildings and animals still in place. In place but all jumbled, because where did they fit without any paths? Nobody knew. And that's how life really is.

Madeleine

Whew, Lord'a mercy! I wisht you coulda seen that face the day it all really began. Homer, he comes stomping into the kitchen, folds up those arms all covered with scratches, and stares at me like he's just set down two buckets of meanness and dares me to say a word.

Howdy, is what I say. I believe in don't go wrastling with alligators if a few steps backwards will do. Which in this case they won't. That alligator goes on and takes its bite. Our young Homer Aldrich Winthrop opens his mouth and calls me an old rat! I am plumb struck dumb, which don't happen but once every century.

But I don't hold it against him, and that's a fact. To Homer, I'm on the side of authority, and authority's just let him down. Which all goes to prove my point: It don't pay to lie or hide things from kids, not even for their own good. Kids deserve the truth. They deserve the knowing of their own history.

Here's how I see Homer right about then: He is laboring for the truth. He is digging and digging and digging, the sweat coming out on his brow. He's dug him a regular trench. I have to stand on the bank with his mother, staring down at the top of his head, being Madeleine, the mean old rat.

But I'm rooting for him, and I think he knows that. I'm rooting, no matter what.

26

That night, I didn't sleep one bit. Well, maybe I did, but it was the kind of sleep where you're still also awake. You know, your brain goes on rolling along with some question or problem, having wide-awake thoughts, but then something bizarre shows up in your head. Like a cabin in the middle of Boston. Or a man with a fancy brain, but it's stuck in stone so he pulls and he pulls and he pulls and he hacks away with a chisel, but he can't *think* how to get it out, so of course he can't. One time a car roared through my bedroom, so I guess I did sleep.

But I must have been making decisions, because when I opened my eyes in the morning, I'd made up my mind. I'd find out what I wanted to know—I'd find out *everything*—but not by asking my mother. I wasn't giving her any more chances to lie or to tell me the truth in some foreign language or to leave out so many major details that she might as well tell the lie. I'd find out for myself.

"Well!" Madeleine said when I came down the

stairs early. "You're looking perky this morning. Are you feeling some better?"

I remembered what I had said to her. You old rat. My ears started burning. How could I have said that to Madeleine? *Madeleine*, who was standing there trying to look happy, trying to pretend things were the same as ever between us.

"I'm sorry," I blurted out. "I didn't mean what I said—well, you know."

Madeleine looked like she hardly remembered and couldn't care less, though I knew that it wasn't true. "Sugar, I know you didn't. And don't you worry. It was a mighty small blip on a mighty big screen. But thanks for saying you're sorry."

That was Madeleine for you. Here she was thanking me.

She made me some blueberry waffles with syrup. I was starving, no big surprise.

"Has my mother listed this house with the real estate agent?" I asked as I ate.

Madeleine looked at me in surprise. "Well, no, Homer, I don't think so. She hasn't been out but that one time."

"She could have done it over the phone." Because this was another decision I'd made: I'd lie down and die before I'd let somebody buy this house. Really and truly. This was a house where I'd been with my father. My father, who *was like me*.

Madeleine shook her head. "Nah. Don't think so."

"She could have. When you weren't listening."

Madeleine stopped what she was doing and stared up at the ceiling, like the answer was written somewhere up there and she was reading it.

"Homer," she said, "your mama's not gonna sell this house."

I couldn't help glancing up at the ceiling. "She isn't?"

"No. Gracious, the very idea's pounding away on the top of her head. Why do you think she's got her this headache?"

I blinked. "Why?"

"Because! Like I said. She's fixing to do what she don't want to do, so her body's aiming to stop her."

Was that how a body worked? Maybe it did, sometimes. I'd already noticed how my mother always got headaches whenever I mentioned the past.

"But what if her body *can't* stop her? What if she thinks she's having that headache because she hates this house so much and so she hurries up to get rid of it?"

Madeleine thought it over. "Could happen, I reckon."

"Well, don't let it." And I was on my way out the door, headed off on my mission.

*   *   *

Roger came to his door wearing yellow pajamas.

"Sorry," I said. Meaning for everything—for seeing you in yellow pajamas, for coming without calling, for running out on you yesterday and not taking your phone calls.

"No problem." He smiled. "I'm just glad you're back."

We went upstairs. I sat on his bed while he got dressed. "Ugh," I said. I pulled a baseball glove out from under me, then a book, then a squashed banana.

"Oops, sorry. I wondered where that thing went." He gave the banana a whiff, then winged it over his head in the general direction of the trash can. It missed. I stopped to wonder for a minute if he really did have a mother and father. Maybe Roger's Law ruled because Roger Sweeney was a king in his own kingdom.

"Man, I was worried," he said. "I thought you were mad at me."

He'd thought *I* was mad at *him*? I shook my head. "Of course not. I just had things I had to think over."

"Such as?"

"Such as, I'm going out there."

He stopped in the middle of putting his arms through the sleeves of a T-shirt. "Out there? To Owl Island?"

"Yes. I'm following Fake Man out on the boat."

I expected this announcement to make Roger happy, but instead he just looked at me.

"So you have to tell me—"

"Don't do it," he said. He pulled the shirt over his head. His hair bounced out of the top of it.

I stared at him in surprise.

"I know, I know, I wanted you to go before. But now I don't." He sat down on the edge of the bed and pulled on his sneakers, then clomped them down on the floor, the yellow laces just hanging there. "It's too dangerous."

I frowned. "Wasn't it always dangerous?"

"Well, maybe. But it feels different now. I mean, before it was sort of a game. Now it isn't. We actually *saw* those smugglers. And if the captain's involved..." He shook his head.

"I don't care."

Roger stared at me as if I had lost my mind, which I guess in a way I had. "Homer, you'd better care. There are slippery cliffs and rocks out on that island. And woods. Fake Man won't stay in the village, you know he won't. If he's stealing something and catches you watching him..." Roger shivered.

"I'm going out there," I repeated.

Roger sighed and flopped back down on the bed.

27

"Okay," he said, after he'd lain there awhile, thinking. "What's the real deal here? I mean, why do you care so much? Because of your father, right?" He sat up.

I stared into bright round eyes, full of a friend's true concern.

"Yes, because of my father."

"Because he might have known Fake Man?"

"No. Because he made that statue." Following Fake Man was just an excuse. Fake Man was almost irrelevant. Though he wasn't, of course. He was a link in the chain of clues.

"I don't get it," Roger said.

And I didn't want to have to explain it. But the real deal, he had said. That's what you owed a true friend. "Roger, how would you feel if you'd never known one thing about your father, and then suddenly you found out that he'd been a lot like you?"

Roger looked thoughtful. "Surprised, I guess. And happy?"

"Yes, but also mad. Because you have to wonder, why hasn't anyone told you? I mean, until yesterday, I didn't even know my father could sculpt. I thought he was a neurologist. And then, all of a sudden, I see this statue that gives me the chills, that makes me think, Wow, the person who made this is saying something to *me*. He sees things the way that *I* do. And it turns out that the person is *my father*?" I felt a lump rising into my throat, but I coughed to get it out of there. I would not cry, I would *not*. I'd just go on and on being angry until anger got me results.

"And not only has nobody ever told me, but someone has worked very hard to *not* tell me. Someone has had headaches and thrown up in her bed to not have to tell me. I mean, wouldn't that make you wonder? And wouldn't it make you mad?" (Enjoying using this word that *Doctor Winthrop* did not approve of.)

Roger nodded thoughtfully. "Well, yes, I guess it would. I guess it would make me furious. It would make me jump out of a window and take off and refuse to take any phone calls. It would make me"— he sighed and looked down at the ground—"want to go out to Owl Island."

"Right. So that's what I'm doing," I said.

Roger thought for a while. "There are other ways," he said finally. "Better ones. For example, you could drop in at the library and corner my mother. You know, just walk up and say, 'Hi, I'm Homer

Winthrop. I hear you know my family. My mother, *Catherine*, sends her greetings.' You know, catch her off guard. I bet that would work."

"No."

"Or we could walk around town asking questions. Your mother said not to go making connections, right? So, let's go make some."

"No." These were good suggestions, but I wasn't taking them. I was going out to Owl Island.

"A ticket costs twelve dollars."

"No problem. I have it."

"And they don't sell them to minors alone." He looked smug at this one. "They won't let you get on the boat."

"So you'll tell me how to get on. You've had a plan all along."

Roger sighed and rolled his eyes. He sat down across from me. He pulled another shoe out from under a sheet. Yellow laces. He checked his feet to make sure he was wearing two.

"I'm going with you," he said.

"Can't. Fake Man knows you're onto him. That's why you needed me in the first place."

He made a face and stuck the shoe back under the sheet. "You know, you're acting just like me," he said.

I smiled. "Cool. Except I don't keep shoes in my bed. So? Tell me."

He sighed again, and then he just gave in, folding his legs underneath him, getting comfortable so he could talk. He looked very businesslike if you didn't notice the pink stuffed pig whose head had popped up beside him. "Okay, you're right, I do have a plan. It's a good one, too. What's tomorrow, Saturday? Perfect. Heather the Featherbrain's selling the tickets. Heather falls for anything. Plus, it's Lobsterfest weekend. It'll be a zoo wherever you look. You'll just be one more animal."

"Thanks."

"You're welcome. So, here's how it will work. I'll get up early, go into the ticket office, pretend to be checking out postcards or something. Just hang around. That way, when the people with reservations come in to get their tickets, I'll hear their last names. Later, you can go in and say you're with the 'so and so' party and you just decided to go so you need another ticket. Heather will fall for it, no problem. You'll have to meet me at, say, nine-fifteen so I can tell you your alias. Let's see, where?" He stopped and thought for a minute. "How about the playground?"

I managed to nod again. I was thinking, Wow, I really am going to do this.

"Homer? Are you hearing me?"

"Yes." But I wasn't exactly sure that I was. I felt far away and kind of unreal.

"Okay then, think about this. What are you

planning to tell your mother and Madeleine? I mean so they won't miss you all day and stuff?"

I came back to earth with a crash. "I don't know," I admitted, remembering Madeleine's check-in rule. I'd have to make up some kind of a lie. A great big lie that I'd have to tell with a straight face.

"Never mind, I'm pretty good at lying, I'll figure that one out for you, too."

And do you know what? He did.

28

"Your mother requests your presence," Madeleine told me at supper.

"Oh. Is that like a royal summons?" Rude, I admit it. And dumb, since I was supposed to be buttering people up, not getting them more upset at me. But I wasn't thinking too clearly. I was this big raw nerve, no brains attached. I'd been this way all day, ever since Roger's.

Luckily, Madeleine smiled. "No. It's like my nice way of saying 'Get your behind on up there.'"

I sighed. "That's what I meant."

The hamburger I'd eaten turned into a rock in my stomach. I did not want to see my mother. Even though I knew that I should. Even though when I did think clearly, I saw that sliding a lie past a person too sick to listen would be a whole lot easier than sliding it past Madeleine. Once it was past my mother, I could just sort of roll it across Madeleine. Yes, I should go see my mother. I just didn't want to.

I clomped my way up the stairs. I clomped into

her bedroom. My mother's eyes were closed. I cleared my throat. The eyes didn't open.

"You rang?" I said loudly. Nothing happened. I glared at the woman who had requested my presence but not stayed awake to enjoy it. Not that enjoy was the relevant word here. The last time my mother had seen me I'd been wrapped up in a blanket hollering "*You* happened, you old witch." My ears started to burn. I'd sort of forgotten that. My own anger was what I remembered. Now I thought about hers. Gulp. I'd better be nice to her. Really, really friendly.

But when I crossed the room and looked out of a window, I just got angrier, because while I was looking the thought came into my head that here was this great view of the harbor and it was wasted on my mother, who kept curtains closed in the daytime. See, light triggers her headaches. Whenever she'd say this when I was little, I'd pictured a gun that shot bolts of lightning, straight into her eyeballs. *Zap!* Another headache. "But that's exactly what it feels like!" my mother had said when I told her about the gun. "That's it exactly!"

I remember how I'd felt sorry for her at that minute, picturing the gun. Maybe a small part of me felt sorry for her right now. But not really. Because while I was staring out the window at that great Maine scenery, I was thinking how my mother might as well be in Boston. She might as well be *anywhere*.

I yanked down the shade. Why was it up, anyhow?

"Homer?" My mother's eyes shot open.

"Yeah? I mean, yes. I'm here."

My mother turned her head and looked at me. I tried to smile and look friendly. I'd have to apologize to her, I thought. For yesterday. I'd have to actually say I was sorry. Well, that would be lie number one.

My mother managed a weak smile. "I wanted to see if you were all right."

Oh sure, I was all right. I had to lie and sneak and do something dangerous because of my mother, but sure, I was all right. "Yes. I'm fine."

"What did you do today?"

I shrugged. "Nothing. Nothing announceful. In case you were worried." Which was another dumb thing to say if you were trying to be friendly. I guess I was out of practice.

My mother stopped smiling and sighed. "Homer, I'm sorry about that. I should never have said such a thing." She leaned forward and adjusted the pillows behind her. Her face scrunched up in pain. "When I get these headaches, I don't seem able to think."

"It's okay," I hurried to say. "I mean, it's all right." While she was being unable to think, there were things we had to discuss. "I'm sorry also. I was very rude to you yesterday. And I'm sorry for that. But I wanted to ask you something. Tomorrow, there's this Lobsterfest thing, you know?" Whoops, don't say "thing," and don't say "you know." "There's a lobster festival. It's up in Briggin's Harbor. There's going to be cart rides from here to there. So, I mean, can I go?" Whoops, don't say "I mean." "I could take the cart ride and stay all day. There'll be games and contests and"—I caught myself before I said "stuff"—"and I could get a lobster for lunch." Best of all, this was true. There was a festival. I just wouldn't be at it.

My mother frowned. "You're going to go by yourself?"

Hmm, now this was a tricky question. Did she want me to say yes or no?

"Yes," I decided. "But it'll be safe, don't worry. I'll just go there and straight back. You'll know where I am for the whole day." Whoa, major whopper! I felt it all the way down to my feet, how I had just crossed over some line into the liars' bigtime. "And I won't go meeting people, I promise."

My mother seemed to wilt. Her body sort of got flat, like there was nobody under the covers. "I told you, Homer. I'm sorry I said that. I want you to make friends. Of course, you shouldn't go talking to strangers. But that's for the usual reasons. I mean..."

I nodded. "I know what you mean. And it's okay. I'll have fun by myself. I just want to go see a lobsterfest."

And I swear, my mother wilted right out of that room. Just disappeared. This tiny voice came floating up out of her bed. "All right, Homer. You may go. And I hope that you have fun. Have fun for all of us."

Which wasn't what I expected. But, anyway, it was a yes.

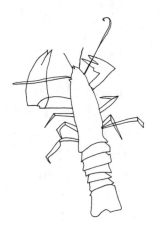

29

That night, I stared up at the turtles.

"You're lucky," I told them. "It's scary down here with no shell."

And I swear, one of those turtles moved. I swear, it did. Okay, I know that it really didn't, but it sure did seem to. Its little feet moved, like a blink.

And that's when it hit me: My father had painted these turtles. Don't ask me why or how I was only seeing this now, but I was. That little turtle was waving its feet and saying: Hey, Homer, your father painted us. He painted us for you.

That's why I could sleep that night when I should have been having nightmares. Owl Island didn't even seem scary. When I went there, I wouldn't be following Fake Man. I would be following my own father. A father who'd painted me turtles.

But by morning, everything had changed. I opened my eyes, and the turtles didn't look friendly. They looked cold and slippery, like the rocks out on that island. The ones you could fall off of and onto.

"A lobsterfest," Madeleine said. "Ain't-choo the lucky duck?"

I nodded and smiled, trying to look like a lucky duck.

"So what all goes on at a lobsterfest?"

"Oh, you know." I took a bite of cereal. What was it Roger had said? "Games, pony cart rides, contests. It's like a fair, you know?"

"Only with lobster for lunch."

"Yep." Yuck. At this particular moment, lobster sounded gross.

"And your mama said yes? She said you could go with Roger?"

Uh-oh. Roger. Madeleine would *want* me to go with Roger. She'd wonder why I wasn't.

"Well," I said. "Maybe I didn't exactly remember to mention Roger to my mother. She probably thinks I'm going alone. But that's not really lying, right? Because she didn't ask, very specifically, 'Is Roger Sweeney going with you?' And I didn't answer specifically, 'No, he isn't.'" Wow, I was getting good at this. Now I was lying about my lying!

Madeleine turned around from the sink. Her hands stopped scrubbing. "You mean your mama would let you go off to a lobsterfest all by yourself when she wouldn't let you go with a friend?" She frowned. Her hands started moving again. *Scrub, scrub, scrub.* That pot was going to end up with a hole in its bottom if it didn't watch out. "Well, you know what? That is a secret I'm willing to keep. I'm *glad* you won't be alone."

I took a big bite of cereal and smiled a puffy-cheeked smile, but Madeleine didn't turn around to see it. Sorry, I said silently to her back.

"You're a Merkle," Roger told me. He looked sort of pleased with the news.

"A what?" Whatever the word meant, it was weirdly like how I felt. Maybe I *hadn't* slept all that well.

"A Merkle. That's your name. The Merkles from Albuquerque bought four tickets for the morning boat, returning on the four-thirty. Two parents and two kids. You'll be kid number three."

My stomach rocked.

"And here, I packed you a backpack. It has binoculars, water, lunch. Who knows when you'll have a chance to eat. I made peanut-butter-and-banana sandwiches. Those were Elvis's favorite, did you know that?" He patted the backpack's flaps and started to hand it over, but he stopped when he saw my face.

"Hey, you gonna hurl or something?"

"No! Of course not!" At least not while Roger was in sight. I stood perfectly still and willed my stomach back into place. I could eat peanut-butter-and-banana sandwiches. I could be a Merkle. I could go off to Owl Island alone.

Roger squinted and stared at me a while. "You know, you can still change your mind. You should just come right out and ask your mother what you want to know. Demand an answer. Have you ever actually done that?"

"No. I'm going out to Owl Island." I reached for the backpack and fastened it onto my back. "Wish me luck."

"Luck," Roger said. I just wished he didn't look like I needed it quite so much.

30

"*What* was the name?" Heather the Feather-brain narrowed her eyes and ran them over the list again.

I snuck a look around. There were tourists all over the shop. "Merkle," I said quietly. Luckily, nobody's head shot up. "The Merkles from Albuquerque. They bought their tickets at nine o'clock. See, at first I didn't want to go, but now I do, so my mother handed me this money and said, 'Well, go on in there and get a ticket.' So here I am." I laid my twelve dollars out on the counter. "I'd been thinking of staying here for the Lobsterfest, but when I saw the boat, I thought, 'No, go to the island instead. A boat ride is much more exciting!'" Stop talking, I told myself. What was the matter with me? It was like I'd *become* a Merkle, I was so strange to myself.

"Oh, yeah, here, I see them. Merkles. On the ten-thirty boat." Heather tore off a ticket.

"Thanks." I stuck the ticket into my pocket, trying

not to rush or look too excited. Trying to just get out of there before I exploded. "See ya."

"'Ya," Heather muttered. I was out of her head already, if I'd ever been in there. Step one completed.

Outside, I shot a look at my house. The windows seemed to look back at me. I had half an hour to wait. I'd better do it someplace else. I wandered up the hill toward the lighthouse. Already, the backpack was growing heavy. I stopped and looked inside it: two sodas, two bottles of water, three peanut-butter-and-banana sandwiches, a package of Twinkies. Potato chips. Chocolate chip cookies. Two apples. Geez, was Roger trying to sink me or something? I decided I'd better start lightening the load if I was going to carry this thing all day. I sat on a rock and ate an apple (apples are surprisingly heavy for being so much like air inside) and drank one of the sodas. Then I ate a few cookies.

I tried not to think about anything. Didn't work. I'd never been on an island, that's what I started thinking. Well, then, my self answered, it's time to go. Pretend you're an explorer, setting off on an expedition. That didn't help either. People died on expeditions. What kind of fool went exploring?

I sighed and picked up the binoculars and looked down the hill. Hey, there was the *Emily Ann*! I could see everything: deckhands moving around on the boat, the antennae on top of the cabin, the flag waving off the back. The sign that said *Emily Ann*. The captain.

A crowd had formed on the docks. I searched it with the binoculars. No sign of Fake Man, but I did see a family of four. Merkles. Or maybe not. There were other families of four, all of them possible Merkles. Not that it mattered. When it was time to get on the boat, I'd fall in with whatever clump of people happened along.

I finished the apple and tossed the core into the bushes where birds could eat it and sighed at the backpack. It was still going to be too heavy. Maybe I should leave it behind in the bushes. I couldn't imagine the me on the island who would get thirsty or hungry. But, I realized, that's because I couldn't imagine a me on the island at all.

Uh-oh. Mass movement down on the dock. People were lining up to get on the boat. I took off running, the backpack jiggling up and down on my back.

When I got near the dock, I stopped. You're Homer Merkle, I reminded myself. Homer Merkle does not have to run, he just has to find his family. At that very minute, a man and a woman came out of the ticket office with two young girls. The mother looked sort of young to be the mother of Homer, but she could be his aunt. I'd always wanted an aunt. Auntie Merkle.

I followed my family onto the dock and looked

around. There were other families, an old man with a dog, people speaking some foreign language (German, I thought), a group of people with Southern accents, a couple of couples, a person who looked like Madeleine, except neat. I did a double take at that one. It wasn't her, wasn't even like her, really, though I'd never seen her when she was neat.

Calm down, I told myself. Madeleine isn't here. But then neither was Fake Man. What did *that* mean?

The captain climbed onto a wooden crate and raised his hands for attention. "Welcome," he said. "Just a few words before we get under way." We all listened while the greetings turned into warnings. Don't smoke or litter or pick any rare vegetation. Don't go out on the rocks on the back of the island where a rogue wave can sweep you away. Don't walk on the black rocks, which are slippery. Don't stand on the edge of the cliffs. Don't do any of the one million dangerous things there are to do. Which might include going anywhere near the captain. I watched his face while he talked. He didn't look like a smuggler, but, of course, that just made him good at his job.

I looked around. Fake Man still wasn't here yet. And part of me, I'm ashamed to admit, felt relieved. But the other part, the part that had sworn to do anything to get at the truth, started worrying. What would I do if he hadn't come by the time they boarded passengers? Should I go ahead and get on the boat?

"And now, welcome aboard!" The captain began taking tickets. I lined up with my family. I decided I should get on the boat. "Owl Island," it had said on the statue. I wanted to see the place. I wanted to follow the trail of my father wherever it led. Anyhow, I couldn't exactly stand around on the dock like some billboard announcing myself: Here I am, Fake Man, ready to spy on you if you show up! I had to stay with the crowd. Follow my family.

My family clattered over the gangplank. Auntie Merkle, my uncle, my two young cousins with bopping ponytails. I clattered behind them. The captain didn't even look at me. I didn't look at him. His hand, when it reached out for my ticket, looked like a normal hand. But what did I expect? A hook?

I followed my family through the closed-in downstairs, outside again to the metal stairs, up to the upper deck, where they fell into seats on the back of the boat.

"Over here, sweetie-pie," Uncle said to his smallest daughter. "I don't want you next to the water." A pony-tailed head sprang up, and I sat down in her seat. I wasn't sure I wanted to be next to the water, either, I thought as I stared through the wire net that served as a railing. For the first time, I wondered about the boat ride. How long was it? Did the sea ever get rocky on days like this? I looked at the sky. It was starting to look sort of fuzzy, like fog might roll in. Fog probably did roll in all the time at sea. I didn't even like boats, really. I wanted off this one! I stood up.

"What are we waiting for?" someone asked.

"Somebody's coming," a Merkle answered. "See? Down there."

And there came Fake Man, moving as fast as a limper could limp, and carrying his cardboard carton.

The captain had held the boat.

31

I watched Fake Man get on the boat. I watched him go into the downstairs cabin. My chest started *thump, thump, thump*ing.

Oops, Merkles. Four sets of eyes were watching me watch. I sat back down.

Fake Man didn't come up the stairs. This was good, I decided. Just as well if he didn't have time to notice me on the boat. The *thump*s settled down, into thumps.

The Merkles all looked away, except for the little girl sitting next to me, who kept on staring. "Are you all alone?" she blurted out loudly. She was probably five or six, but her eyes looked forty. They looked like Madeleine's.

I managed a smile. "No. My mother stayed downstairs. She doesn't like it up here. She gets seasick."

"Oh. She's a weenie. Like my sister."

Auntie Merkle frowned down at her daughter. "Meghan, that's a very rude thing to say!"

Meghan smiled brightly at this information. She

went on smiling while the captain came upstairs and went into the little cabin up in the front. She smiled while the boat's horn blew and the boat pulled away from the pier, her eyes never once moving off my face. Smiling and staring. I sighed. Leave it to me to sit next to Miss Eyeballs.

But when we headed out to the sea, I forgot Eyeballs Merkle. I forgot everything. The boat picked up speed. Wind whipped past my ears. We passed the lighthouse, sitting out on the rocks like a dream floating by. We passed islands, islands, and more islands. Islands were everywhere, big ones and little ones, the ones farthest away looking blue with a layer of mist swirling around them. Now I hoped that there *was* mist on Owl Island. I wanted to experience it!

And I swear, I'd forgotten Fake Man. That's how I am when I see something beautiful. For the whole time I'm doing it, nothing else matters or comes into my head, I'm just a goner, a useless goner, and I don't even care.

But then Fake Man came up the stairs, and I noticed that, all right. *Clomp, clomp, clomp* went his shoes on the stairs and my heart in my chest. He was heading straight toward the captain's cabin. But he went past it, up to the railing in the very front of the boat. I watched, sort of hypnotized, to see if the wind would blow off his fake hair, but he pulled out a baseball cap and clamped it down, hard, then put his hand on top of the hat.

Hey, where was his cardboard carton? He must have left it down below. But that was probably because it was empty. A person heading out to smuggle things wouldn't have the goods with him, going out. He might have the tools of his trade, whatever those tools would be. But even an empty box would be a clue. An empty box would, in fact, be evidence!

"Excuse me," I said. Miss Eyeballs lifted her legs and let me go by, the tips of her sneakers *whoosh-whoosh-whoosh*ing against my pant leg. Homer the Spy hardly noticed. Homer the Spy was in a hurry to get down those stairs and check out the carton while Fake Man was still up here.

I found the thing at once. It was sitting right up front in the inside cabin, on top of two other boxes, its top unsealed, its flaps simply folded over. I stared at it for a while. In two seconds, I could flip up those flaps and look inside.

There was only one problem. This cabin was full of people. I couldn't just walk in and open the carton. Okay, here's what I would do. I'd go in, look around for a seat and not find one, then just sort of sit on the carton. No, not sit, lean. I'd lean and then, after a minute, the box would start to slide, so I'd have to grab at a flap to catch it. Whoops! I'd say as the flaps came unfolded. Then, while I was folding them back up, I'd check out what was or wasn't inside. Easy as pie. And fast.

And it all went just like I planned. That is, up to the sliding part. When I got to the sliding part, I looked around to make sure no one was paying attention. And no one was. No one had even noticed me come in. Then I gasped. Oh yes, someone had. There, in the back of the cabin stood Fake Man. Looking straight at me.

Okey-dokey, I thought, keep cool. Don't do anything stupid. You're just a kid leaning on some boxes. But you might want to lean sort of lighter. I slid my elbow off the carton.

Fake Man stayed exactly where he was standing. I stared out at the water.

"Hey!" someone hollered. "Seals!"

Everyone rushed to the windows, me included, but my eyes weren't seeing the seals. They were looking out the back of my head, watching Fake Man watch me.

"Cool!" a boy said to his father. "I want to go outside." So did most people, it seemed. The rows of seats suddenly emptied. I sat down by a window and pressed my nose up against it, but my eyes were in shock. I couldn't see a thing—not water, not sky, not Fake Man's reflection in the window. Was the man even still in here? I didn't know and didn't plan on turning around and looking. I planned on sitting exactly like I was sitting for the rest of the ride.

Which took forever. Forever and forever. After a

while, I thought if I didn't move soon, my neck would crack and my head would fall over. I pictured it hanging there like a flower on a broken stem. People were moving around behind me, coming inside, sitting down. Suddenly, I couldn't stand it a minute longer, not any of it. Not the sitting perfectly still, not the wondering if Fake Man was in the cabin. I just turned right around and looked. He was gone.

Gone where? To tell the captain not to let me off of the boat? Gulp! I'd be left alone with the captain and crew. I went back to sitting perfectly still, trying to disappear.

That carton was still up front, but trust me, I wasn't touching it.

32

It turned out to be good I was in the cabin. When the boat finally docked, I was the first one off of it. Nobody tried to stop me. I started walking, not even looking behind me. There was only one path, a bumpy dirt road leading up to the village, and Fake Man would have to take it.

I passed a line of pickup trucks waiting to carry baggage, passed a crowd of people who'd come down to meet the boat (or to take the return trip home—I didn't know, didn't care, didn't have time to wonder), passed fishermen fishing off the docks, passed a big old building set up on a grassy hill that had people sprawled all over it. I kept on going, walking, knowing that he was back there. He was back there, and he was coming. Fog drifted through the woods ahead of me, and this fog looked creepy, not cozy like the fog back in Herring Cove.

Roger was right, I decided. I shouldn't do this. Forget following Fake Man. I would just stay in the village and look for clues to my father.

But how could I not follow Fake Man when I'd come this far? And Fake Man *was* a clue to my father.

I sighed and kept moving.

In the village, I had to choose: left or right. I stopped. Ahead was a store with a picture window. Perfect! That window looked straight down to the water. I could watch from inside, see which way Fake Man chose to go. I opened the door and went in.

"Help you?" asked a pony-tailed man.

"Oh, no thanks. Just looking." Which I made myself take a minute to do. Hey, this was an art supply store. I felt a buzz of excitement. Maybe I *should* just stay here and look and forget following. I could get paints in this store.

The door suddenly opened. "Hey, Charlie, how goes it?"

"Same old, same old," answered the pony-tailed man.

I looked up. Fake Man! Fake Man was right in this room, holding his cardboard carton. How had he gotten here so fast? He must have been right behind me. Was *he* following *me*?

I looked back down. I opened a box of colored pencils. Twenty colors. Twenty colors with two unusual blues, yes, that was cool, and please let my face have no expression except that I liked these colors. I closed up the box again. My hands were shaking.

"I'll take another tube of that yellow you talked me into."

Charlie chuckled. "Thought you'd go for that." He came down the aisle. Passed me. Rounded a corner and returned with a tube of paint.

"Thanks. Put it on the bill. I want to get out there before the fog lifts."

"Yep. Catch ya later."

Fake Man was gone. Quickly, I reached into my pocket and pulled out money to pay for the pencils.

"These are good ones," Charlie said. "Subtle selection of colors."

They were! For a second I wished I could stay there and talk about colors, but I couldn't. I had to see what Fake Man had rushed off to do in the fog.

"You an artist?" Charlie asked as he handed me change.

Now this made me stop and think. I thought I was an artist, but to an artist, I probably wasn't. "No, not really. I just like to draw things."

Charlie laughed. "Sounds like an artist to me."

"Was that an artist who was in here just now?" I slipped the pencils into my backpack. I was pleased with the way I had asked it, like it was just something to say, not something that really mattered.

Charlie didn't answer. I looked up. He was leaning against the wall, his arms folded on his chest, squinting at me suspiciously.

Whoops. I managed a smile and threw my backpack over my shoulder. "Later!" I called as I went out the door.

Fake Man was nowhere in sight, but he couldn't be far, he'd only just left the shop. I looked left and right. I chose left and set off running. I'd try one way and then the other.

I saw him almost at once. He was walking along the road, moving fast (no limp!), carrying his cardboard carton.

I slowed down. I looked at the fronts of some houses, looked into the windows of shops. Tried to act like I came here often and knew where I was going.

"Hello," I said to a stranger.

"Morning," the stranger answered.

We passed a church and a little green—the place where my father's statue had stood! I wanted to stop, but Fake Man was moving even faster. I'd come back later. If that statue had stood on this green, then probably my father had stood here also. My feet felt happy and safe just walking across the grass. When the path wound past an inn called The Trailing Yew, I couldn't help smiling. "Hint, hint," I called softly to Fake Man, who had disappeared into the woods.

Uh-oh. Woods. I stopped walking. Forget happy and safe. But this wasn't really woods, I told myself. Just a woodsier part of the village. I peered through the trees and saw a fence and a rooftop in there. I made myself keep going. There went Fake Man, around a bend in the path. Already, my legs were starting to ache, and the backpack was getting heavy. At least Fake Man hadn't taken one of the paths that led off to the left, which headed straight uphill into fog-topped trees. This path went uphill, but slowly. It stayed in what seemed to be village, though the houses were getting farther and farther apart.

And slowly, the path got narrower. It climbed over some rocks, snaked through a woods. Fog drifted across it. Now there weren't any houses. Sometimes I saw Fake Man, and sometimes I didn't.

Man, where were we going, anyway? And what would we do when we got there? I didn't know. The thought made my legs feel like Jell-O. My knees actually shook. For the first time in my life, I wasn't noticing beauty. The woods were just woods that had danger and mystery in them. I could pretend as much as I wanted to, but the fact was, I hated danger. I thought about this as I walked. Really, who doesn't hate danger if they like being alive? It was a no-brainer.

I wiped the sweat off my forehead and shifted my backpack. What I was doing was crazy and stupid. The smart thing to do, the brave thing, even, would have been to do what Roger had said: just confront my mother and ask what I wanted to know. Look her right smack in the face and demand an answer. So what if her head boinged up to the ceiling? I wouldn't look away. That was the kind of unpleasant and scary experience you'd at least live to talk about afterward.

Suddenly, the path came out of the woods, into a clearing. Ahead, fog floated out over rocks—fog that was more like a mist. Mist, as in water? This must be the end of the island. There were probably cliffs out there, but how would you know where?

You win, Fake Man, I thought. Because my feet wouldn't go any farther. They were bolted right to the rocks. Wherever you're going, you're going alone.

But he wasn't going anywhere. He was standing right behind me. He grabbed my shoulder, and I whirled around, and there he was! The brave new Homer Winthrop fell to his knees and yelped like a dog.

We're All Shook Up!

The funny thing was,
the Homer that was part me/
part him was braver
than the me that
was all me.

He was awesome!

A superhero!

Hey, I think. _I_ want to do
something brave! I want to help
Homer solve his mystery. I decide
I'll go into that cabin alone.

That sounds brave.

So I do. Sort of.

I'm halfway inside
when I get busted.

When I find out who Fake Man is,
I know we're in trouble big-time.
Next thing I know, I'm spilling
the beans.

Singing like a canary.

Ratting on Homer.

Oh great.

Way to be brave, Roger.

Sorry, Homer.

But it turns out Homer was getting busted right about then, too.

We are two slick dodos — I mean dudes.

33

I wish this story could be different. That I could say I did something brave. You know, like leapt to my feet and assumed the Kung Fu position. Demanded to know all secrets! Here's what I really did:

I started shaking.

Begged, "Don't hurt me!"

Fake Man raised both his hands and backed off. "Hey, I'm not trying to hurt you. I just want you to 'fess up. What are you following me for?"

He stared, and I stared back. Stared but didn't breathe. Didn't breathe, couldn't breathe, might have been about to fall over.

Fake Man sat down on a boulder. He folded his arms. "All right, that's okay. I can wait. You let me know when you're ready to talk."

I would, I would let him know. It didn't feel like anytime soon.

"For crying out loud," Fake Man said, starting to look angry, "this just burns me up, it really does. All of it."

All of it? I hadn't done enough to be clumped into an all of it. Had I?

"I'd like to know what I did to deserve this never-ending, gol-darned, infuriating total invasion of privacy. To warrant a *spy*, for pity's sake!"

If I was quick I could run, I was thinking. Make it back to the village.

"Don't even think about it," Fake Man said.

So I stopped. But the fact was, I could run if I wanted to. Now Fake Man was frowning up into the sky, not even worrying about me. When I struggled onto my feet and brushed the dirt from my kneecaps, he hardly even noticed. But, of course, his not noticing made me not need to run. It made me want to stay. Grill him with some questions.

"I mean, what's the big deal here?" he asked the sky. "What is it people want from me?"

"Well, *I* want to know why you're wearing a wig and makeup," I answered, suddenly finding my voice. "Why you're sneaking around. *I* want to know what you have in that box."

Fake Man looked at me in surprise, then he blinked a few times. "What I have in the box? Why? What do you think I have in it?"

I blushed and shrugged. "Something suspicious." Which sounded dumb, I know.

Fake Man snorted. He leaned down and flipped up a flap of the carton. "Here, see for yourself."

I leaned over and looked. And I have to tell you—Well, really I can't tell you, because what I saw doesn't have any words. Not any real words that go deep enough.

Because what I saw was a painting. The most beautiful painting—the most beautiful anything—I'd ever seen. It was a picture of fog. Fog and the tip of a rusted old metal shipwreck, which seemed to be creeping in through the mist, crawling up onto the land, filled (you just knew) with an army of ghosts.

And no words can tell that, not exactly the way I saw it. I felt sort of dazed, as if I'd fallen into the painting and was wandering down through the fog, down, down toward that rusty old shipwreck. If that painting had whispered, "Homer, follow me anywhere," well, I'd be there.

"Hey, kid!" Fake Man reached out an arm and grabbed me. "No noseprints needed, thank you just the same."

I pulled myself up and tried to shake off the man's fingers, but I still felt far away.

"You all right? What's going on here? What were you expecting?"

I stared at the man. "Did you paint that?" I managed to ask.

"Sure I did. Or I am painting it, I ought to say. I can't seem to get it right."

I watched while he lifted it out of the box and

leaned it against a rock. He hadn't gotten it right?

"The wreck is that way." He sighed and nodded toward the fog moving over the rocks. "If we stay here long enough, it'll come wavering into sight. I ought to be getting set up. If you plan to let me."

But he wasn't really thinking about me anymore, I could tell. He had pulled a folding easel out of the box. Then oil paints. Then a palette and paintbrushes and rags and an empty tin can for his turpentine. He was thinking about his painting. Mumbling questions to himself, such as, "Does that fog have too much gray in it? Maybe it needs some blue?" I knew exactly where his mind had gone off to. It was the same place mine liked to go.

This weird idea came sort of drifting into my head, creeping around like the fog. I felt it before I thought it.

"Okay, so what are you wondering now?" Fake Man asked. He was squirting paint onto his palette and swirling it with his brush. I watched his face while he worked. He wasn't the least bit scary. Why had I thought he was?

"I'm wondering what I said before—why you wear a disguise. And why you try to look old when you're not." But that wasn't all. I was wondering what the idea floating through my brain would look like if I stopped it from drifting and made it just sit there and line up and be facts. So I did. Here's what those facts looked like:

1. My mother had known Fake Man.
2. Fake Man had known her.
3. They were both in hiding.
4. Fake Man was an artist.
5. My father had been an artist.
6. Fake Man went back and forth to an island where my father had stayed or worked or at least visited before he died this mysterious death that no one would tell me about.

So then, *Fake Man could be my father*. A father who hadn't really died, which is why no one would talk about it.

Fake Man stopped swirling his paints. "Look," he said.

I looked. The fog was lifting. The tip of the rusty old wreck came poking its nose into view, arranging itself on the rocks as if posing for its portrait. I watched, knowing the ship wasn't really moving, that that part was only illusion.

Fake Man could be my father. Was that an illusion also? Or was it a fact that could sit there and be a truth when the fog finished lifting? For that one minute, I picked truth. For that one minute, I had a father.

34

"So," Fake Man said with a sigh. "You want to know why I wear a disguise."

I watched his paintbrush dabbing away at the painting, but I wasn't really seeing it. My heart was pounding so hard it was about to jump out of my chest. It was a new and bigger pounding than I'd ever had before, even when I was running. I nodded and managed to croak out, "I know you're actually young."

Fake Man smiled. He reached up a hand and pulled off the wig. "Young, I don't know about. Middle-aged, I'll confess to."

I studied his head to see if it looked like my head. Maybe.

"All right, look here, sonny, I'll tell you. But you have to promise to keep my secret."

"I will," I whispered, wondering if he knew who *I* was. Because he wouldn't tell me if he did know. Would he?

"You ever hear of a painter named Owen Castle?"

I nodded. "Sure." Owen Castle was famous. It was like asking if you'd heard of Elvis or Michael Jordan.

"Well, sonny, that's me."

I know my mouth fell open. I know my eyes bugged out. I know I seriously popped some brain cells because here's the ridiculous thing I said: "My *father* is Owen Castle?"

Fake Man stared at me in surprise. "Your *father*? Kid, what do you mean by that? I'm nobody's father, believe me."

And my hopes just sank. They clunked with a thud from my heart right into my stomach. Because I did believe him. I could see the truth on his face. And I guess he could see the truth on mine. He saw how much I wanted a father. How I wanted one so badly I'd have taken a man who wore a disguise to hide from his own wife and son. At that moment, I felt Fake Man look right into my heart, like I had no skin or bones on, seeing the real and pathetic me.

Fake Man didn't comment. I mean, the man didn't even ask questions. He just pressed his lips together and squinted and went back to his painting.

"But the wig—?" I said. "The disguise—?" I was feeling how those things had worked to trick me. That this wasn't all my fault.

Fake Man, aka Owen Castle, sighed. "The price of fame. You know what happens when people know I'm around?"

I shook my head.

"They follow me wherever I go. They stand there and watch me paint."

I stopped watching him paint. Or at least I tried to.

"They ask me questions and offer critiques." He shook his head. "You won't believe what just happened to me in Florida. I was working on an island sort of like this one, and word got out that I was around. Cripes, I started painting inside a cardboard carton, to keep people away. Now wouldn't you think a box would offer a hint? Privacy desired. Well, guess what? People just came on around and stared into the carton. 'Hi,' they'd say. 'You must be Owen Castle!' The thing was just a billboard: Here sits Owen Castle!"

He stopped talking and stared at his painting for a while. "This picture is making me crazy. Nothing I do to it makes it right."

"It already is right," I told him. "It's perfect." Then I blushed. Uh-oh. Was that offering a critique?

If it was, Owen Castle didn't look mad. He looked interested. "Why do you say that?"

Well, gulp. I mean, I didn't know how to explain it, it was just something I felt. But the man was watching me, waiting for an answer. Which I wanted to give if it would keep him from changing the picture. I thought for a minute.

"Okay. You know how when you draw something

just right, it looks like the thing you're drawing, but different? And how it's what's different that makes it the reason you wanted to draw it in the first place?" But was this really true, or was it just true for Homer Winthrop? I looked at Owen Castle, whose face had gone sort of blank.

I tried again. "Like, say you're drawing a picture of someone who's handsome, but he's also mean. So, you start out making him handsome, and you're drawing along and drawing along, but then the first thing you know, you've made some little part of him ugly. Somebody else might think you got that part wrong, but you know you didn't. That part's just told you the one thing you needed to know. Or something like that."

"Or something like that." The man's voice was flat. I didn't know what the flatness meant. But he didn't look annoyed. He still mostly looked blank. And maybe sort of surprised. He puffed out his cheeks and exhaled in a little explosion. "Okay then, how does that make this perfect?" He pointed to his canvas.

I held up my hands and bugged out my eyes. No way was I going to discuss Owen Castle's paintings with Owen Castle!

"Really," he said. "I mean it. I'd like to hear what you have to say. Trust me, I wouldn't ask if I didn't."

So I took a deep breath. Stared at the painting

again, then out at the wreck, which seemed to wink at me through the fog. "Well, you sort of painted in all of the ghosts. Or the feeling of ghosts. And you made it feel like the ship is trying to creep up onto the land, like some giant pathetic old—old—lobster or something that's been in the sea too long. It's wounded. It's going to die. This was its last chance, but it didn't work out, so now it's really sad. Not only sad, though. It's also happy, I don't know why."

We both looked at the painting awhile. Owen Castle was quiet. I snuck a peek at him. He was sitting there perfectly still, his face a blank.

"So sure," I went on, "it's a painting of a rusted old ship, but it's *not* a ship also. And it's the not-the-ship part that matters. And...And...Well, I don't know what else to say. Or how you did it." My voice dropped off to a whisper. "I only know that you did. And that I don't want you to change it."

Owen Castle looked up at the sky. When he looked down again, he had tears in his eyes.

35

We were quiet a long time. I stared out at the fog, which seemed to be lost and wandering. It drifted out over the sea, it drifted back on the land. Fog seeking a home.

"Sorry," I said finally.

This weird kind of snort—might have been a laugh, might have been a cry—came out of the man. I snuck a peek at him. He had pulled a handkerchief out of his pocket and was wiping it over his face. "Cripes, kid. You've got me ruining my makeup." He held the handkerchief up. It was all gooey and pink.

"Sorry," I said again.

Owen Castle dropped the handkerchief into the carton and sighed. "Oh, don't be sorry. Can't say I remember when I last felt so happy."

Happy?

Owen Castle chuckled and looked at the painting again. "A pathetic old lobster. Well, what do you know about that?" He shook his head.

My face started burning. "But I didn't mean—" Though of course I had meant that. I'd meant it exactly. "I only—"

"Don't explain yourself, son. You said it right the first time. Hey!" Under the smear of makeup, his face got all pale with excitement. "Would you take a look at that!"

I looked. A man and his dog had stopped to examine the wreck. The dog had his nose in the air. He was sniffing, looking excited, like he'd picked up some great new scent.

"As if it's a carcass, right?" Owen Castle looked excited himself. He grabbed his paint brush and opened a tube of paint. "As if he's caught a whiff of a dying old *something*!"

I opened my mouth, but it was no use. He was already at work, swirling paint around on his palette, squinting up at the scene. Nothing I said was going to stop him, I could tell by his face.

Squeeze, mix, dab, dab. And there came the dog— head, body, tail. Part of me hated watching, but another part had to. It was a great dog.

The real dog had stayed for only a minute, but Owen Castle kept squinting at the wreck like it was standing right in front of him. I think he'd forgotten that I was there, which was fine by me if being forgotten meant being allowed to watch. I tried not to move, even when pins and needles shot down my legs, and my rear end went to sleep. Even when I got thirsty and hungry and had to go to the bathroom.

"There," the man said suddenly, stepping back from the canvas. He tilted his head to the side. "There you have it."

Yes, he had it. But what was it?

"Life sniffing the air at death," he said, exactly as if he'd heard me. He smiled and wiped his brush on a rag, then dropped it into the jar. "Sniffing the air and feeling uneasy, but then passing right on by. Going off with a wag of the tail. Because, really, what else can a puppy dog do? That ship's not going to get up and float again."

He threw the rag in the box and gathered up all of his paints, carefully twisting their tops back on. His face got serious. "Still, you have to sniff at a shipwreck. You have to respect that it's there. That it floated before it sank. That it carried real people." He sighed and stood up, and for a long time he just stood there, being perfectly still, staring out at the sea. "Yes," he said finally. "Sniff, but then wander on. Because you cannot live on a shipwreck."

I didn't know what to say or if I was even supposed to answer.

He suddenly turned and smiled at me. He put a

hand on my shoulder. "So. What's the verdict here, kid? Did I ruin the picture or not?"

"Not," I admitted. An artist this great probably couldn't ruin anything. Whatever he painted would just be great in a new way. And there would always be lots of ways—the painting with the dog, the painting without it, both of them seeming perfect. Both of them being perfect, only in different ways.

"Good. Glad to hear it." Owen Castle looked happy. "Hey, there wouldn't be lunch in that backpack, now, would there?"

I unbuckled the backpack and pulled out the sandwiches. Then the chips, the cookies, the sodas.

Owen Castle laughed.

"Roger," I said. "My part—" Whoops! "I mean, my friend." I blushed and handed the man a sandwich. "He packed me this backpack."

"Ahh, yes, Roger." Owen smiled. "He of the big rubber bands."

Now, what could I say to that? I took a big bite of sandwich. Banana stuck to the roof of my mouth.

"What's your name?" Owen Castle asked while we ate.

"Homer. Homer Winthrop."

The man's mouth dropped open so fast it was like he had sprung some hinge. His hand let go of his soda. Coke spilled over his pant leg and onto his shoe. He didn't even notice. "No," he whispered. "It can't be."

"Well, yes, it can," I said. "I'm Homer Winthrop's son."

It sure felt strange saying those words. You know why? I had never once said them.

36

"Heaven help me!" Owen Castle was staring at me. "I can't believe that I didn't see it! You look just like him. You are just like him. That whole speech could have come straight from your father's mouth. I guess in my mind you were still a baby. I mean, I saw your mother this week in the village, but—"

"I don't believe it," I said.

He looked at me in surprise. "You don't believe what?"

"That I look just like my father. That I *am* just like him." The trouble was that I *did* believe it. For the first time in my life, someone was telling me the truth about Homer Winthrop, which was letting me see how big the lie had been. "Somebody would have told me. I would have known it! Right?"

Owen Castle frowned. "Well, you would think so. Didn't your mother—?"

"No. She didn't." And that pretty well summed up my mother. She didn't. "My mother hardly even talks.

She's just a rotten useless old...headache. She hasn't told me one thing about my father."

Owen Castle's eyebrows shot up. "Really? You mean that quite literally?"

"Yes. Quite literally. Well, okay, maybe not *literally*. She's told me one or two things. Like that my father was a neurologist who died of a neurological illness. And that he came from Cleveland. But that's all. That's what I know about my own father. Now I'm not even sure if those things are true, because I also know that he made that sculpture back at your cabin and painted some turtles on my bedroom ceiling, so I'm thinking that he was an artist. Right?"

Owen Castle was quiet a long, long time.

"Right?" I repeated. "And I *am* like him?" I already believed it, but I wanted to hear it again.

Owen Castle stared down at his sandwich. Then he said in this quiet voice: "Yes, son, you are. You're very much like him. Even as a baby, you were. Your father used to brag about that. He loved you like crazy. I can't believe that you haven't been told. And yes, he was an artist. An artist *and* a neurologist."

My father had loved me like crazy! I wanted to stand on a boulder and pound my chest, I wanted to cannonball off a cliff, but I just sat there trying not to move so the truth wouldn't notice I was there. I knew all about the truth—how it can bolt just when you're ready to grab it.

"Your mom has never remarried?" Owen Castle said after a while.

"No." I scowled. Now, really, who would marry a headache? "And I don't want to talk about her. Or, yes, maybe I do. What I would like to talk about is: What is the big fat secret she carries around in her head?"

He ran a hand over his face, smearing his makeup. "I believe I can answer that, Homer, but it isn't my place to do it." He wiped the hand on his pant leg, leaving a pink streak.

"Well, whose place is it? My *mother's*?"

He sighed and looked me straight in the eye. "Okay, look. I'm going out on a great big limb here. I'll tell you what you want to know. I hope you're ready to hear it."

"Of course I'm ready to hear it!" But the man's face was scaring me. I hoped that I *was* ready.

He smiled a sad kind of smile. "Your father was an artist, just like you guessed. I remember those turtles. But I can't believe that's all you've seen of his work." He shook his head. "That and the statue. The statue isn't typical. Your father was first and foremost a painter. And he loved to draw."

Like me! "So there's a lot to see?"

"Oh yes, there's a lot. And don't worry, you'll be seeing it. A group of us are renovating that old cabin. The one I believe you've already seen?" He paused to raise an eyebrow at me, but I was too busy imagining seeing my father's artwork to feel embarrassed. "We're going to turn it into a kind of gallery/ museum. Your father's work will be front and center. We all have paintings and drawings of his. He gave them away like they were nothing when they were gems, every one."

"He was a very good artist? As good even as you?"

"Oh, he was better than me. He was better than any artist I've known. Sure, some of us have exceeded him over time, but that's only because he quit. I never got over that, how someone like Homer could quit."

"Why did he? Because he got sick?"

Owen Castle sighed and stared down at the ground. "No, Homer. He quit long before he got sick. He quit to go to med school. Then he met your mother, and they got married. I decided right off that she was the enemy—you know, it was her fault he sold his soul to his doctoring and let his painting become a hobby. But why should I presume to know a thing like that? Your parents lived down in Philadelphia. I didn't witness their life. In fact, I didn't know your mother. Not in a way that mattered."

"Well, I bet she was the enemy! I bet she told my father, 'Forget that dumb playing around with paints!' Only she'd have said it in fancier words. Like—like— *Labor omnia vincit!* Or she'd have looked at his paintings and not said a word! Probably dropped them right in the trash can when he wasn't looking!"

Owen Castle smiled. "My imagining exactly. So whenever they'd come up here on vacation, I'd say, Homer, remember the light! Meaning the light out here on the island. We'd lived here together, you see. Two whole years before he went off to go to med school. Man, what I learned in those years." He shook his head.

"And what would he say?" I asked. "When you would tell him that?" I was looking around, thinking, My father has seen that wreck! Has seen this exact view! Has maybe sat on this very rock!

"Oh, he'd just laugh. The fact was—" Owen Castle suddenly stopped talking and set down his sandwich carefully.

"What? *What* was the fact?"

No answer.

"The fact was what?" I demanded in my most kick-at-the-seat voice.

He looked at me. "The fact was, your father seemed happy. No, your father *was* happy. He was a brilliant doctor. And you know, I can see it now, how he was using his skills—those steady hands and his all-seeing eyes and his gentle nature. He was doing something he loved. I chose to ignore that. No, I did worse than ignore it. I resented it. And when he got sick and you all moved back here..." He looked up at the sky. His makeup had caked into a ring around his neck. "Oh, Homer, it's something I can't even say."

"Well, you have to say it!" I couldn't believe it. Here went the truth, getting ready to run again! This time I'd chase it. This time I'd stomp on its weasly guts!

He closed his eyes. "I convinced him he needed his art." Like this was some major pronouncement. Like we could just hang him now for his crime.

"Well, of course he needed it! What's the big deal in that?"

Owen Castle shook his head. "No, he didn't. He needed rest. And peace of mind. And your mother. She blamed me for the way he died. And you know what? I think she was right."

I shot up off the rock. "*What?* My father died of a neurological illness. How could that be your fault?"

The eyes opened and turned to look at me. The look in them was a look I had seen a billion times. Sadness, I thought. Sadness just like my mother's. The kind that was trapped deep down inside a person. The kind that could never escape but only peek at you out of the person's eyes and make you wish you had never seen it. Maybe you *hadn't* seen it, that's what you told yourself later, when really, you knew you had.

"No, Homer. Your father *had* a neurological illness. That isn't how he died."

Meaning what? I hated in advance whatever he was about to tell me, but I knew that I had to hear it.

I wanted to hear it. I'd been waiting my whole life-time. But waiting for something, even wanting it, doesn't mean you'll be ready when it gets there.

"Your father killed himself. At the cabin."

The words sat there like big black lumps.

Like I said. Waiting—even wanting—doesn't mean you'll be ready when something comes.

Madeleine

Great day in the morning. Let me tell you, this story has a happy ending, but it took some doing getting there. Took the day of great revelations. The day a policeman arrived, dragging that new friend of Homer's, who'd gone limp and loose as a dishrag and twice as sorry-looking.

"This young man would like to inform you of something," the policeman says to me very politely. "Are you Mrs. Winthrop?"

"No," I answer. "I'm not." And I just stand there, dumb as a post, till finally I remember to move my feet and climb up the stairs to get Homer's mother. It's when I look in her face that I see what it is I'm thinking: Homer must be in trouble. I tell you, we're back down those stairs in a New York minute.

"We caught this young man breaking into the cabin up by Pauli's woods," the policeman informs us. "It seems he and your son have been working on solving a mystery: Who's the man in the bad disguise? Well, I can tell them. The man's Owen Castle. And he happens to own that cabin." He shoots Roger a look, then turns to the doctor. "Your son, however, madam, is doing his detecting out on Owl Island. I thought you ought to know that."

"Owl Island?" Dr. Winthrop's face goes white as a new-washed sheet. "You mean today? You mean right this minute? Homer's out on Owl Island?"

"Oh, he's not just out there. He's following Owen Castle. Which, trust me, will not make Mr. Castle happy."

Dr. Winthrop is plumb struck dumb. She stares at Roger, who's looking down at the floor, but you can see how he's feeling her eyes on top of his head. His face turns as red as his hair.

She turns and stares out the window, like she can see all the way to the island, like if she's quick she can will Homer back. But she sees that she can't, so she turns around again.

"Why, Roger?" she asks.

Roger sneaks a peek upwards and shrugs. "Well, at first it was like a game. Until...until..." He stops talking. Looks back down at the floor.

"Until what? Please, Roger, I'd like you to tell me." And she's not sounding mad, she's sounding sad, like all she wants is to understand. Which I reckon is all she does want, her not being able to will her son home to her.

That Roger, he tells her all right. He spits out the whole story in one big long breath like it's been burning a hole in his belly. "Until Homer saw that statue at the cabin and how it was signed with his father's name. His name and 'Owl Island.' Which made him really mad! Because he loved that statue, and it showed him how his father was a lot like him and he didn't even know it, or know anything about his father, since you wouldn't ever tell him. And he decided Fake Man, I mean Owen Castle, must have known his father, because you acted so spooked when you saw him, like you knew who he was. Then you told Homer not to go making connections, and my mother said, 'Keep Homer away from that cabin!' and that was our final proof that there was some kind of a mystery. A giant mystery. And it had to do with you. And the cabin. And Fake Man. And Homer's father."

Roger stops and takes a breath. Dr. Winthrop falls backward, into a chair. The woman is downright speechless. Well, I reckon we're all speechless.

Except the policeman, of course. "So," he says, "naturally, the first thing you would do when your mother says 'Keep away from the cabin' is head right for it."

Then this magical thing happens. Roger's chin and shoulders go up. His eyes get all fiery. I see that the boy is handsome. That under that shock of hair, he has a fine and noble brow. "Yes," he says, "it is. Because after that, it wasn't a game. It was a very important questing! A questing for Homer's father." Those were the words he used. A very important questing. Don't that just beat all?

"And I wanted to help in that quest. I think Homer was brave to go out to that island. It's the bravest thing of all to do something when really you're scared! Which Homer was. After he got on the boat, I thought, Wow, *I* want to do something brave. I decided the best clues were probably right here in town, were probably in the boxes in that cabin, which we hadn't even bothered to look in because Homer got so upset and ran. So that's why I broke in. It was going to be a surprise. Like a present, for Homer. And you know what? I'd do it all over again. I would, I really would! Because Homer is lonesome, and you can tell. Everyone needs a father. Or at least the memory or story of one. And I don't think it's right that you never tell him!" Then he looks smack-dab at Dr. Winthrop. From the mouths of babes, I tell you.

The doctor stands up, sort of weaves around, reaches out for the back of her chair. She doesn't say one word. Well, mercy, what can she say?

After that, the policeman takes Roger away, and there's nothing to do but wait. Homer will be on the boat that gets in at five-thirty. I try looking busy, but really I'm not. I'm keeping an eye on the doctor. I don't like how she's gone all pasty and won't talk. She broods for the live-long day.

"Oh, Madeleine," she says, along about three-thirty. "Haven't I been a fool?"

Now, what can I say to that? Why, yes, madam, you have! You've been a fool in many areas! No, thank you. I reckon I'll keep my mouth shut. Anyhow, what do I know? It's too easy to say what other folks ought to be doing or ought to have done in some situation. Walk a mile in their shoes, then maybe you'll know. Dr. Winthrop's shoes would cripple me in a heartbeat, those pinched-up little feet. I believe the woman has never once had on slippers. I swear, she has not. I bet not even owned a pair.

"Take off your shoes," I tell her. "Let's give those toes some air."

That's advice I am comfortable giving.

37

*O*wen Castle's face was the saddest face I'd ever seen. Sadder even than my mother's. "I'm sorry, Homer," he whispered.

I didn't answer. Couldn't answer. I didn't know what to say. Or think. Or do. *At the cabin*, that's what my brain was saying. Like that was the part that mattered.

"It's a shock, I know. But trust me, he only did it because he was dying. And a miserable punishing death it was. Homer was a doctor. He knew what was in store for him and for you and your mother. He saw it as kindness, I truly believe that. But your mother didn't see it like that. She saw it as abandonment. Your father left her before he needed to go."

Suddenly, this picture rose up in my head. It was an awful picture. I wanted to throw it right into my suitcase, but my suitcase wasn't there. Where was my suitcase? I saw my mother standing alone on the doorstep waiting for my father to come home. She waited and she waited and she waited, but my father didn't come, and he never would.

Owen Castle was staring at me. "I'm sorry, Homer," he said again.

I nodded. "But I still don't see how that was your fault." My voice had this funny rasp, like it was somebody else's. "You didn't tell him to do it. Right?"

"No, absolutely not! But I did tell him to start painting again. 'It will be therapeutic!' I said. And, you know, for a while it was." His eyes got bright, like he was remembering something happy. "Your father cheered up. His illness improved a little. 'See, it's the painting!' I told your mother. 'It's feeding his art-starved soul!' Being my usual know-it-all self."

"Maybe it was," I said, thinking how if *I* were sick and going to die—if I had to pick one last thing I could do—I'd make a map showing a road from earth up into the sky. I'd paint it with bright colors. Make the sky a Maine blue. Just doing that would make me happy, I believe this to be true.

"Oh, maybe a little at first. But then it started causing him so much frustration. His hands weren't steady. His eyes were going blind. I'd fired up his artist's longings when he could hardly hold a brush. Looking back, it seems downright cruel. You know what I think now?" His eyes roamed around on my face like they were looking for something but didn't know what.

I shook my head. Artist's longings? I was thinking. I'd never heard that expression before, but I knew right away what it meant. It's what I'd seen in the eyes of that statue.

"I think that more than he needed his art, your father needed his family. His wife. And we shut her out."

I frowned. "Shut her out how?"

"Oh, you know. We formed a unit that didn't include her. She didn't understand about art. Or rather, she didn't understand the artist part of your father. But she understood other things. Things that maybe I didn't. I just didn't want to admit that. So whenever the path led back to your mother, I stuck out my foot and got in the way. Homer, what a thing to have to say. I've had years to think about it, and I know what I did. I see it so clearly now."

"But you were only trying to help," I said. I felt sorry for him. He looked so broken. But *I* was seeing something clearly, too. I saw my mother alone on the doorstep.

"Yes. But it wasn't the right help. Or even my place to do it."

We didn't talk for a long time. There were so many thoughts and emotions bouncing around inside me, I couldn't focus on any one of them.

Suddenly, Owen Castle smiled. "I wish your father could have heard you talking about my painting," he said.

"Why? What would he have said?"

"He'd have said, 'Well, well, well. My son is an artist, how about that?' And he'd have been incredibly proud."

I stared at him in surprise. "How do you know I'm an artist? You've never seen me draw."

"Being an artist isn't about drawing, Homer. You know that. It's about *seeing*. That's what made your father so brilliant. He had a genius for seeing. For observing detail, you know?"

Yes, I did, I knew.

"I swear, he could look at a hundred details and pick out the one that mattered the most, the one that told the truth."

My ears started tingling. My father had painted, and his paintings told the truth. I wished I could have known him. I wished I could have seen him work.

"But you know what? You don't have to paint to be an artist. An artist simply *is* an artist, down in the depths of his soul. It doesn't matter what it is he's doing. You carry that greatness inside you. I wish I'd said *that* to him," Owen Castle whispered. "I wish I'd understood it when he was dying."

We sat there in silence, our impossible wishes sitting beside us. Sniffing at shipwrecks.

38

The trip home sure was different from the trip over. Owen and I stood in the front of the boat, staring out at the water. Somewhere behind us sat a family of Merkles. I'd seen Meghan get on the boat.

"Hi, cousin!" I'd said. She'd stuck out her tongue in a friendly manner.

"Look, over there!" Owen pointed into the distance. A school of porpoises was breaking through the water. "Beautiful," he said, shaking his head in appreciation. "Your father loved seeing porpoises. Back then, there was only the mail boat out to the island. Sometimes the porpoises would leap up not twenty feet from the boat."

"Wow!" This day is a dream, I was thinking.

He stopped talking and looked straight at me.

I tried not to laugh. His wig sat on his head like a hat, tipped sort of crooked.

"Well, Homer," he said. "What's going to happen when you get home?"

I felt the smile fall off of my face. Good question.

"You'll tell your mother, that's what I'm imagining. You'll tell her how you met me and how I told you about your father. Then I guess we'll both be in hot water. But that's all right. I believe it will be for the best."

I tried to imagine telling my mother about Owen Castle. Discussing my father's dying. Not likely. Suddenly I didn't even want it to be likely. Because now that picture of my mother was changing. She wasn't standing on that doorstep alone, she was going inside, where she had a son. And what would she do when she got there? Nothing. Not even give him a hug. "Maybe I won't tell her. Why should I? What did she ever tell me?"

Owen Castle sighed and looked down, into the water. "Okay, Homer, here I go again. Out on another great big limb. But there's something else you should know."

I stared at the back of his crooked wig. Now it didn't look funny at all. It looked sort of weird and scary. Like there was some unknown creature underneath it that was getting ready to stick out a claw.

"You hate your mother, I know. I even understand it. In some ways, what she's done is inexcusable. It makes me so angry, thinking of your not knowing your father. Not knowing how much he loved you. But, Homer, your mother went crazy with grief." He looked at me again. "And I mean truly crazy."

Well, this was no big surprise. My mother was still crazy.

"She went into this kind of stupor where no one could reach her. Do you know the word catatonic? I think that describes it. They put her in the hospital, and she stayed there a long, long time."

A hospital? A feeling of panic rose up in my chest. "Did I go visit her?" I asked. But he didn't have to answer. I knew. I saw my mother in a bed in a white room, looking far, far away. Looking invisible.

"I suppose you did at some point. Maybe when she was recovering. I don't know for certain. I wanted to visit her myself, but I was the last person she'd want to see, assuming she'd even know me."

"She wouldn't have known you?"

"Well, no, son, probably not. That's what a stupor means. Your mother lost touch with reality."

"She wouldn't have known me, either?"

"Well, you know, I didn't see her, so I can't really

say. Most likely she did. I mean, you were her baby. But, Homer, if she didn't, it wasn't her fault. She was just lost for a while, that's all."

"So what happened to me?" I asked. "Where did I go?"

"You and your nanny stayed at the house. The town really rallied around. Gave you your birthday party. Your third, I think it was. They felt so sorry for you. For that matter, they felt sorry for your mother. It was just a tragedy, Homer, all of it. I hoped your mother would find some peace, but from what you say, it sounds like she never has. That's why, well, all of it. You know? That's how much your mother was hurt. And, I imagine, why she still can't talk about any of it."

Me and my nanny had stayed at the house. Suddenly, like the ocean rising up and smashing right over the railing, this wild cold feeling washed over me. Because now I was remembering that, I was sure I was. How I'd been a child who'd been left behind. My parents had rowed out to sea in a boat and left me alone on the shore.

"Maybe I shouldn't have told you," Owen said.

This was really a question, I knew. He wanted me to tell him it was all right. I didn't say anything. I didn't know what to say. I didn't know if it was all right. I was too sad to talk. I was sad in a way I had never been sad before, or at least I had never admitted it.

He sighed and shook his head. "Honestly, the things I do with my good intentions. I'm sorry, Homer. I just wanted you to understand about your mother—how a person doesn't have much say on where grief takes him in his life. It's taken me to some pretty strange places. God only knows where it's taken her."

I knew where it had taken her. I saw it, clear as a bell. Her grief had taken her inside her own self and locked her up tight, and she couldn't get out, not even when she wanted to. And she did want to, I decided. She wanted to, but all she managed were pasted on smiles and pretend cheerfulness when she tried.

We were passing the lighthouse. Two dogs ran back and forth on the rocks. We were getting close to Herring Cove.

"Uh-oh," Owen Castle said when the boat chugged up to the dock and swung around. He pulled the wig from his head and nodded toward the landing.

I looked where he was nodding. There stood my mother and Madeleine!

Uh-oh was right. "Man," I said. "She's going to kill me!"

But I could see by her face that she wasn't. She didn't even look mad. She looked scared. And she looked little. And she looked sad, just like me.

Doctor Winthrop

I should be prepared, given the hours I've had to reflect, but my son's face on that boat is the face of his father — his father with Owen Castle — and this shocks me anew. I don't want to remember. I won't.

I force myself to look. Homer's face is small and his eyes are hollow. Lonesome, Roger has said, and I see it to be true. It makes me ashamed to the depths of my being. My child is an orphan.

But Owen Castle puts a hand on Homer's shoulder and the boy stands upright. I see that he has survived. He has stepped up into the world out of a parentless childhood. Good for you, Homer, I think. You've pulled anchor and sailed beyond me. It may be the first unselfish thought I've had in all my years as a mother.

But Homer's boat isn't leaving, it's coming closer. The sprit of its bow is pointed toward me. Watching, I feel the strangest emotion start up in my chest. It is then that I know. It is then that I see: my son still needs me. He's coming home, not going away.

Return to Sender

Everybody knows that facing the
music doesn't really mean cops.
It means mothers.

Mine talked her way through her crisis. She talked to my father and her friends and the town selectmen. Talked to every single person who came into the library.

The theory was,
    I could be explained.

So my mother forgave me.
   Homer's forgave him.
His mother forgave me.
   Mine forgave him.
Madeleine forgave everybody,
but she probably wasn't mad
in the first place. Owen Castle
said the next time we want to
visit the cabin, bring a hammer
  and do some work. And leave
the rubber bands at home.

Homer and I are best friends
because that's how it is when
  you've been blood brothers —
you stay blood brothers
                    forever.

Audience may applaud no

39

The statue now sat outside, by the front door of the cabin.

My mother was staring at the statue in exactly the same way I had, as if she were hypnotized. What was *she* seeing? I wondered.

Finally, she pulled her eyes away. The eyes looked tired. Plumb wore out from looking, Madeleine would have said if she were here. "But I don't understand," my mother said. "How could Homer possibly have done this when he was dying? He was so weak. Well, I guess he didn't manage...I guess he died before..." Her voice cracked.

"Oh, no, Catherine! Homer carved this when he was young. When we were working together out on Owl Island."

Yes! It was all I could do not to let my fist shoot up in the air. I had known that, how this statue wasn't about dying. It was about living. About trying to be born. "And it's finished, too," I added.

Owen raised his eyebrows at me in surprise. "Yes, it is. It's finished."

"But those eyes," my mother said. "They're so full of misery. I just assumed . . ." Her chin began to tremble.

Owen nodded. "That it was Homer's final misery. Well, sure you would."

"But see, they're not about misery," I hurried to explain. "They're about wanting to *see*. About wanting to understand things and about how sometimes you can't, no matter how hard you look and think, but you have to keep trying anyhow."

Owen Castle smiled at me. I could tell he agreed. "This is quite a kid you have here, Catherine. He's certainly his father's son."

My mother looked at me. "Yes," she said. "He is. Oh, Owen, you should have seen how well he could draw when he was just a little boy. It used to break my heart. I wanted so much for Homer to be there to see." Now she *was* crying. She turned her back on both of us. She pulled a tissue out of her purse and wiped at her eyes. "I have those pictures put away in a drawer. I saved every one."

I couldn't believe it. Which drawer? I'd have demanded if I could speak.

"After a while he stopped showing me," she went on. "That was just like his father, too." She turned around and stared at the statue again. She sighed.

"Not that Homer actually stopped showing me his paintings. He simply stopped expecting me to comment. My comments were too inadequate. It was frustrating and embarrassing. Here I was—*a linguist!*—not knowing what to say. Yet what can a layman say in the face of such profundity?"

"So you liked the paintings?" I asked, just to be clear.

"Of course I did! And your father knew that. But you...Homer, a little boy's paintings should hang on a refrigerator. I...They..."

We stared at each other awhile. Then we all turned and looked at the statue, as if it might say what we needed to say.

"You know," Owen Castle said, "I believe there *is* misery in those eyes, along with the rest of it. Homer was a very compassionate man. He felt people's suffering deeply. That's how he could paint them with such feeling."

"Yes." My mother nodded. "And how he could be such a fine doctor."

Owen took hold of her hand. "Catherine, I'm sorry. Homer loved you. He loved you and his child more than anything on this earth. I should never have come between you at the end of his life."

There was a funny sound in my mother's throat. The hand that was free flew up and pounded against her mouth and then just stuck there. She didn't move or say a word. It was as if she'd turned into stone. Put a bun on my father's statue, and it could be my mother.

For one minute, the thought made me angry. I wanted that statue to be about *me*. Me and my father, the artist who understood me.

I stared at the statue. The statue stared back at me. And all of a sudden, a different feeling rose up in the anger's place. It was my artist's longing. There was something I needed to draw. Something hard, maybe impossible. I didn't have a clue how I would do it, I only knew that I needed to try. I needed to get down on paper how that statue connected everything. All things happy and all things sad. The people who lived and the people who'd died. The things you could know, the things you couldn't.

My father. My mother. Me.

Dear Elvis,

Wow, I can't believe it. Your book was the best Christmas present I ever had—the best *any* kind of present! I'm going to keep it forever to remind me of you and Maine. Not that I need reminding! I hope you don't mind that I showed it to Madeleine and my mother. It had us all laughing and saying how you are a comic genius. (My mother says there's probably a better word for your type of genius than that, but she can't think what it is. I'll let you know if she figures it out, which she will.)

Madeleine wants me to tell you she doesn't look like your picture of her anymore. She's got a new haircut. Now she looks more like a Brillo pad, which, she says, moves her one step closer to being a 100% lean, mean, cleaning machine. But your picture really quacked her up. You can see that she hasn't changed, except for that haircut.

My mother *has* changed. She's not exactly a regular person, but I think there's hope. She looks me in the eye. She answers questions. Her bun's not so neat!

We'll definitely be coming up there next summer. My mother's going to help set up the museum at the cabin. All this time, she's had these great drawings and paintings my father did locked up in storage, and, Roger, you should see them! Well, you *will* see them. My mother's donating them to the museum, except for one she's letting me keep. It's of me as a baby, though I don't really look like a baby. I look like a pile of circles and triangles and squares with a curl on top. Hey, I was a cute baby!

Thanks again for the great present. I hope you liked the picture I painted for you. In case you didn't know, those two objects sticking out of the cabin's windows glowing like stars are supposed to be the bottoms of your big old feet as you're crashing through!

Your best friend,

Homer

So many people have helped me along the way with this book. I wish to thank, first and foremost, my editor at Knopf, Nancy Siscoe, my husband, David, and my daughter Sarah, all caring, gifted, and thoughtful editors. A number of friends, primarily Amy Edgar Sklansky, Jody Staton, and Jana McCann, read drafts of the manuscript and offered excellent suggestions. And thank you to my son-in-law, Steven Margulis, for the Elvis sandwiches.

This book would never have existed had my husband and I not purchased our own chopped-in-half house in Maine. I want to thank all of the people who helped make that happen: Olivia Way, who first sent us to Maine; Cap de Rochemont, Kathleen Wright, and Lida and Malcolm Morley, who made the purchase a possibility; Ken Anderson, who looks after our house when we're not able to be in it. And, last but not least, thank you to all of the people who make Maine magical for us and who allowed me to ply them with questions and snap their photographs while I was creating my fictional Herring Cove: Doug and Verena Anderson, Pat and Ernie Roebke, Jane and Ed Ingalls, Robert and Eloise Ensor, Georgia Hansen, Norm Tate, Polly Lantz, the Cushman family, Betty Wilson, and Captain Jim Barstow, to name but a few.